DEADLY WITH

The Vice-President pulled out his putter. It went *Whisk! Whack!* furiously, narrowly missing Chiun on both swings.

"Be careful, Little Father," Remo hissed. "He's really, really fast."

"No one is faster than a Master of Sinanju," Chiun cried as his nails began weaving a defensive pattern around him.

The Vice-President cocked his club again, and Remo saw his chance. He plunged in, his hands reaching for the Vice-President's smoothly tonsured neck.

Remo's fingertips brushed the Vice-President's neck hairs. Then, so quickly that he could not believe it, Remo was holding empty air . . .

. . . and was hurtling directly into the path of Chiun's deadly flashing nails!

#82

The DEStroyer

SURVIVAL COURSE

Created by
WARREN MURPHY & RICHARD SAPIR

A SIGNET BOOK

SIGNET
Published by the Penguin Group
Penguin Books USA Inc., 375 Hudson Street,
New York, New York 10014, U.S.A.
Penguin Books Ltd, 27 Wrights Lane,
London W8 5TZ, England
Penguin Books Australia Ltd, Ringwood,
Victoria, Australia
Penguin Books Canada Ltd, 2801 John Street,
Markham, Ontario, Canada L3R 1B4
Penguin Books (N.Z.) Ltd, 182-190 Wairau Road,
Auckland 10, New Zealand

Penguin Books Ltd, Registered Offices:
Harmondsworth, Middlesex, England

First published by Signet, an imprint of New American Library, a division of
Penguin Books USA Inc.

First Printing, October, 1990
10 9 8 7 6 5 4 3 2 1

PUBLISHER'S NOTE
This is a work of fiction. Names, characters, places, and incidents either are
the product of the author's imagination or are used fictitiously, and any resemblance
to actual persons, living or dead, events, or locales is entirely coincidental.

For Captain Jack Deveny, with thanks.

And for the Glorious House of Sinanju,
P.O. Box 2505, Quincy, MA 02269

1

Not everyone agreed the President of the United States should go to Bogotá.

A Pan American drug summit was scheduled for the next day in Bogotá, Colombia. The embattled President of Colombia was the host. Leaders from as far north as Canada had already arrived. All that remained was for the President's arrival, which everybody did agree would be a tremendous show of support in the long war against the Colombian drug cartels.

The polls were evenly split on the matter. It was a hot topic on radio call-in shows, Sunday-morning TV information programs, and in bars. In Washington, politicians debated the subject with unusual intensity. Only the White House staff was unanimous in its support of the President's brave decision. In public.

In private, it was a slightly different matter.

"For the last time, you gotta cancel!" pleaded the President's chief of staff. "Tell them you have the flu."

"I'm going," the President said firmly in his slightly nasal voice, a voice that mixed New England consonants with a Texas twang. When excited, the President sometimes sounded like an out-of-tune steel bango. He was not excited now. He was firm.

"I'm going," he repeated firmly.

"The drug barons are blowing up buildings all over Bogotá," the chief of staff pleaded. "This thing is a security nightmare. If we postpone it—just postpone— there's time to work out a change of venue. Relocate the thing to Texas, or even northern Mexico. Say, Nogales. On the U.S. side of the border."

"How would it look if the President of the United States bowed to the threats of these narco-terrorists?" the President demanded. He was seated at a kidney-shaped desk, trying to finish a thank-you note.

"A damn sight better than if the presidents of Chile, Peru, Ecuador, Canada, and Mexico all ended up in body bags—provided there are any nonliquid parts left over to bag," the President's press secretary said pointedly.

The President stood up. Outside the family compound in Kennebunkport, Maine, a Marine helicopter was whining to life, ready to ferry the President to the waiting *Air Force One*.

"No," he said, "I'm going to Bogotá. Now, you two get on the train or stop playing with the whistle."

"If we can't talk you out of Bogotá, how about we move the conference to another Colombian city?" the chief of staff whined. "Just to throw those narco-thugs off-balance?"

"Can't," the President said irritably. "You know that. The other delegates are already settled in."

"Think of your family."

"I have. And of millions of other families wounded by drugs."

"Then think of the Vice-President in your job!" the chief of staff blurted.

The President stiffened. He adjusted his glasses. His voice grew chilly. "He's a good man. He'll grow."

The chief of staff subsided. "Fine," he grumbled. "Let's hope if they do bomb the conference, they do it before you get there."

"Let's hope they don't do it at all," the President added pointedly, reaching for his blue poplin windbreaker with the presidential patch.

At Massachusetts' Hanscom Air Base, where *Air Force One* was being refueled, the topic of the President's trip to Bogotá was on the lips of the ground crew as they pumped Jet-A fuel into the thirsty 707's fuel tanks.

"He's crazy to go," said a corporal as he kept one eye on the truck's gauge. The fuel truck resembled a common oil truck that delivered fuel oil to residential homes. Except it was shorter and painted a military gray. "Those Colombians, they're cold," the corporal added. He snapped his fingers. "They'd snuff him out just like that."

"He's committed," said the other, an airman. "He can't back down now. He'd lose face."

"Better to lose a little face than have your legs and everything between them blown away. Know what I mean?"

"If we back down to these scum, they'll only get braver," the airman retorted, frowning in perlexity at the round grille he suddenly noticed under the fuel intake. He could have sworn it hadn't been there a moment ago. "We'll lose Colombia, then Peru, and the rest of South America. How long before Mexico is run by drug lords? Then what do we do? Build a fucking wall like the East Germans?"

"We execute the pushers in this country, that's

what. Dry up demand, and those bastards are out of business."

"You know," the airman said in a funny little voice, "I could have sworn that grille wasn't there a minute ago."

The corporal looked up. He noticed the chrome-ringed mesh grille. It looked like a tiny speaker.

"What do you suppose it is?"

"Probably some electronic sensor or something. This bird is loaded with the latest electronic warfare equipment. What I'm wondering is, how come she's drinking so much fuel? We've been here quite a while."

"That's what I was thinking too." The corporal tapped the gauge. The pointer stayed where it was.

"If I didn't know better," he muttered. "I'd say we just pumped in more fuel than this bird's capacity."

"Well, you know *that* ain't so."

"Yeah, you're right. I guess we were jawing when we should have been paying attention. Ah, there it goes."

A little cough-syrup-red fuel sloshed back from the intake and the corporal hurriedly threw a lever, cutting off the flow. He pulled the nozzle from the intake and capped it.

"I still think the President is a fool for going," he added, dragging the hose back to the truck. "Prestige is important, but survival's what counts."

"That's what this is all about, America's survival."

Together they retracted the hose in silence, and then drove away.

After they were gone, the chrome-ringed grille retreated from sight and the white metal skin healed over as if from a wound.

In the cockpit, Captain Nelson Flagg was running

through the preflight cockpit check with his copilot. The damper switch was stuck.

"Hit it again," the copilot said.

The captain did. A telltale amber light came on.

"This thing hasn't been right since eighty-eight," he growled. "I can't wait until the replacement comes in."

"They should have retired this bird years ago. It guzzles gas like a Cadillac, the controls are finicky, and she burns oil like a Sherman tank."

"Just a few more months. If they ever get the wiring fixed in the new bird."

"Yeah. And if we survive this trip. I don't know about you, but I belong to the club that says the President is a fool to go."

"I'll be sure to pass your vote along to the chief executive if he pokes his head into the cockpit. You got the booster pumps?"

"Center off, main on," said the copilot, unaware of the chrome-ringed microphone disk that appeared on the floor beside his shoe like a metallic eye opening. It had appeared, as if on cue, when the copilot uttered the word "survive."

Then the clatter announcing the arrival of *Marine One* and the President caused them to forget their argument and focus on the remainder of their flight-line check.

Hours later, over the sparkling blue of the Gulf of Mexico, Fort Worth air-traffic control handed over *Air Force One* tracking to Mexican air-traffic control in Monterrey.

"Here's where it gets hairy," Captain Flagg warned his copilot. "Just remember. These Mexicans traffic controllers may sound like they understand English, but half the time they don't catch what you're saying. Ask 'em if we can put her down on an oil platform in the Gulf and they'll happily roger the request. Or as they say, 'royer' it."

The copilot laughed. "It can't be that bad."

"They also like UFO reports. Report an in-flight problem and they ask you to confirm it as a UFO sighting. And that's just Mexico. It'll get worse the further south we go. Listen."

Captain Flagg hit his throat mike and began speaking.

"Monterrey air-traffic control, this is *Air Force One*. Over."

"*Air Force One, we welcome you into our airspace. Say your heading.*"

"*Gracias*. We're proceeding on a southerly course to Mexico City."

"*Royer.*"

The captain flashed his young copilot a lopsided grin.

"Royer," he muttered.

As the Gulf fell behind and *Air Force One* came in over the Mexican coast, the copilot looked down. Barren ranges of mountains rolled under the starboard wing, looking for all the world like a herd of dusty brontosauruses had collapsed and petrified there a million years ago.

"Brrr. I'd hate to have to ditch down there," he muttered.

"Royer," Captain Flagg said, laughing.

The U.S.-made Stinger missile destined to bring down *Air Force One* was built in General Dynamics' Pomona Division and shipped via the CIA to Pakistan and then across the Khyber Pass by pack mule to the Afghan Mujahideen. It lay for an entire winter in a cold cave controlled by the Hezb-i-Islami faction, along with three others, until it was finally brought into service.

A Soviet MIG Flogger was sweeping the desert floor and a rebel commander ordered it shot down. A goatherd-turned-freedom-fighter named Kaitmast brought the Stinger to his shoulder, uncapped it, exposed its optics, and braced himself for the blowback.

The Stinger sat on his ragged shoulder like a length of inert pipe.

Hastily Kaitmast thrust it aside and brought another to his shoulder. That one ignited, sending a rocket racing for the Flogger's glowing yellow tailpipe. The Stinger was designed to home in on the craft's superhot tailpipe. This one instead went crazy, zigzagging all over the sky like spastic skywriting.

The MIG vectored away. The Stinger gave a last sputtering gasp and dropped straight down, denting the top of a mountain.

Kaitmast cursed and drew back a boot to kick the dud Stinger in frustration. His rebel commander stopped him with a word.

"No," he spat. "We can sell it."

Back to Pakistan went the Stinger, where it was bartered to representatives from Iran for AK-47 ammunition. The Iranians, in turn, passed it along to Shiite fighters in Lebanon, where, after a complicated series of events, it fell into the hands of Bishara Hamas, a.k.a. Abu Al-Kalbin. In English, "Father of Dogs."

Among Palestinian terrorists, Abu Al-Kalbin was not a major player. Unlike some terrorists who pretended to be committed to Islamic revolution—and not merely murder and money—Abu Al-Kalbin was for sale to the highest bidder. It was that simple.

But when your *nom de guerre* is Father of Dogs, bids are usually low, even if you do have possession of an operational Stinger missile.

So when the Cali drug cartel of Colombia contracted with Abu Al-Kalbin for his services, Bishara Hamas indulged in no rug-merchant bazaar bargaining.

"Whatever is it, we—my Krez militia and I—will accomplish it," he confidently told his potential employer over a bottle of Omar Khayyam in his Beirut apartment.

The man who called himself "El Padrino" was dark of complexion, with the shiny black eyes of an Arab. But he spoke with a Spanish intonation as he carefully explained what he desired.

It was nothing less than the extinguishing of the President of the United States.

"Done," said Abu Al-Kalbin, who hated America because all his friends did.

And so it was that the Father of Dogs found himself, with both members of his ragtag Krez militia, crouched in the chilly top of a bare Mexican mountain in the desolate Sierra Madre Oriental range, beneath the air lane where their employer had assured them *Air Force One* would travel.

The hours dragged by as his men shivered and examined their precious Stinger—now nearly five years old—as if it were their firstborn.

"Put that down, you donkeys!" Abu Al-Kalbin snapped. "It is our only one. If you damage it, we will forfeit our payment. Worse, the prize we have sought for years will never be ours."

The men hastily lowered the Stinger to a blanket, careful not to jar it.

Abu Al-Kalbin brought his night-vision glasses back to his eyes. He had been told to look for an ordinary 707 flanked by F-14 Phantoms flying escort.

He frowned, thinking once again how the escort complicated matters. What if he knocked down one of the Phantoms? No, the heat-seeking missile would seek the closest heat source, the multiengined 707, not the fighters flying high cover.

The night wore on. He wrapped his kaffiyeh more closely around his mouth. He had worn it for disguise purposes—not that he expected to be spotted in this desolation of mountains—but the high thin air was chilling. His stomach rumbled hungrily, and he thought of the *tostada* he had bought from the street vendor back in Mexico City, only hours before.

He hoped he would eat again soon. Decent food. There were Arabic restaurants in Mexico City. He contemplated a feast in the best of them before the night was over. Lamb. Or stuffed pigeon. Perhaps *sorrit issit* for dessert. And a bottle of Laziza beer.

Then all thought of his next meal departed Abu Al-Kalbin's thoughts. They careened back to the *tostada* as, suddenly, urgently, he felt his bowels gurgle in warning.

"I suddenly do not feel well," Abu Al-Kalbin said slowly.

"What is wrong?" asked Jalid.

Abu Al-Kalbin did not answer. He was looking about the barren mountaintop for a bush or shrub to go behind. But there was no vegetation to shelter his modesty.

"I have the *turistas*," he moaned. "I must do my business here. Both of you—turn your backs!"

And as he began to drop his pants, a distant drone cut the night. Abu Al-Kalbin blinked.

"It comes!" a voice shrieked. It was Walid.

"Not now!" Abu Al-Kalbin cried, his eyes sick as they lifted to the star-blasted Mexican night. "You cannot come now!"

But it was coming now. Just as the smelly contents of his bowels were abruptly erupting onto the ground.

"You must do this yourselves," Abu Al-Kalbin moaned. "I am helpless." He moaned like a wounded cow, seeing his chance for immortal glory running from him like the hot contents of his digestive tract.

His men fell onto the Stinger. They fought for the honor of being the one to bring the hated American President down in ignominious flames.

"One of you! Just one!" Abu Al-Kalbin shouted.

Walid wrestled the Stinger from his fellow, Jalid. He hefted the clumsy black tube to his shoulder, removed the cap—which came off too easily, he thought—and sighted.

"I have it!" he shouted, spotting *Air Force One* in the optical sight. It was a winged shadow studded with lights.

"Do not hesitate! Launch!" Abu Al-Kalbin shouted, his face miserable with shame.

Walid triggered the Stinger. The protective tube kicked, expelling its contents. The first stage carried it away. The second stage ignited, sending it screaming into the night like a Roman candle.

At his electronic nest aboard *Air Force One*, Electronics Warfare Officer Captain Lester Dent spotted the heat source far below. Then the radarscope picked up an incoming object.

"Something coming at us," he shouted to the flight crew. "This sucker is traveling!"

"Disengaging autothrottle," Captain Flagg said, taking the plane off autopilot. He took immediate evasive action, hitting the right rudder. The big four-engine jet heeled sharply.

"Deploying phosphorous bombs!" Dent called out. From pockets in the aircraft's skin, phosphorous bombs were ejected. They ignited, providing convenient targets for any heat-seeking device.

Unfortunately, the five-year-old Stinger, improperly stored and manhandled for much of its life, was not homing in on anything in particular. It zigzagged for one sputtering phosphorous bomb, careened past it, and vectored back in the direction of *Air Force One*.

"Monterrey ATC," Captain Flagg called urgently. "I have a problem."

"Royer. Are you declaring emeryency?"

"Affirmative, Monterrey. Advise we are at thirty-two thousand feet and taking evasive maneuvers to evade unknown approaching object."

"Are you reporting UFO?"

"No, dammit. I don't know what this thing is!"

"UFO. Royer, Air Force One," Monterrey said laconically.

"Dammit," Captain Flagg muttered, feeling the flying wheel go stiff in his hands. "Oh, my God!" he said.

"What?" gasped the copilot.

"The wheel. It's not responding."

"Hydraulics are fine," the copilot said, looking at his array of warning lights. They were amber, not red.

"It won't move."

"I'll try mine."

Before the copilot could take over, his flying wheel moved of its own accord.

"You got it?" the captain asked.

"No."

"What?"

"I'm not touching it," the copilot snapped. "See for yourself."

Captain Nelson Flagg looked over to the copilot's wheel. It was moving to port, putting the aircraft into a slideslip.

"What the hell is happening here? She's flying herself."

"Let's try to bring her back together."

The captain and the copilot put their shoulders into it, trying to hold their wheels steady. The wheels moved as if unseen hands had control of them.

"No go!" the copilot said in defeat.

"This damn ship!" Flagg grated.

Then he forgot all about his cursing as a sputtering incandescent object shot up past their windscreen and, turning sharply, came right at them.

The elevators abruptly moved of their own accord, throwing *Air Force One* into a steep dive. The approaching rocket disappeared from view.

"I lost it!" the copilot barked, craning to see out his side window. He caught a flash of one F-14 coming around, and only then became aware of the pilot's anxious chatter in his earphones. He ignored it, thinking, where'd that bogey go?

Then a flash of light burst off to starboard. The aircraft shuddered and the controls seized up.

Three red lights lit up, accompanied by the engine-fire warning bell, shrill and insistent.

"Number four engine," the copilot called hoarsely. "EPRS on one, two, and three dropping fast."

"Fire the bottle and shut it down," Captain Flagg

said crisply. Into his mike he said: "Monterrey. Monterrey. This is *Air Force One*."

"*Royer. Go ahead.*"

"I am declaring a special emergency at this time. We're going to have to make an emergency landing in the desert."

"*Royer. Happy landings, Air Force One,*" Monterrey said unconcernedly.

"Did he understand what you just said?" the copilot asked Flagg.

"No," returned Captain Flagg, looking down at the intensely black wrinkled mountains that were coming up to greet him. He hit the ident button, which automatically doubled his radar blip for Monterrey's benefit, and switched the transponder to emergency frequency. He wondered if it would matter.

In his private compartment, the President of the United States had already assumed the crash position —crouched over, hands on ankles and head between his knees—when he heard the mushy *whump!* of the explosion.

It had all happened so fast. A steward had come in to say there was a problem. That was all his Secret Service guards needed. They were on him like reporters, practically smothering him with their bodies, pistols raised ineffectually, looking at one another in sick fear.

"What was that?" one croaked.

"Explosion."

"Oh, dear God, no."

The President heard them as if through a curtain of roaring in his ears. He was thinking that this was a highly undignified way for the leader of the free world to die. He felt the blood rush into his brain as the craft began to plummet.

He wondered if he would black out before the worst came. In his mind's eye he could see the seats in front of him accordion toward his helpless fetal-positioned body, the way he knew they did in airline crashes.

Crushed between airline seats. It was a ridiculous way for a President of the United States to die, he thought again.

And then he felt the seats in front of him press against the back of his neck, pushing his chin back into his seat. He didn't hear the horrible sound of impact, and he wondered why. In fact, he felt no fear. Only the comforting warmth of the seats around him as they pressed protectively against his coiled body. He felt safe. It was an odd feeling.

Then came a sudden jarring and the President of the United States thought no more thoughts.

2

His name was Remo and he was trying to convince the guerrilla leader that, despite his UPI credentials, he was indeed an American spy.

"You admit this?" the guerrilla leader asked. He wore a colorful poncho over striped trousers. His tall charro hat was the least riotous bit of his costume. He looked like an Incan cowboy.

They were in the heart of the rain forest. Monkeys and macaws chattered in the distance. Remo, whose white T-shirt and black chinos were not exactly jungle attire, nevertheless did not sweat in the Turkish-bath atmosphere. Instead, he was idly wondering what the dozen or more members of El Sendero Luminoso were thinking of. As guerrillas of the Mao-inspired Shining Path revolutionary movement, they were dressed for moving unseen through a piñata forest, not a Peruvian rain forest. Or were piñatas Mexican, not Peruvian? Remo had no idea. He didn't get down south of the border much.

"Sure," Remo said nonchalantly. "I admit it. I'm an American spy."

"I do not believe you," the guerrilla leader—whose name was Pablo—said flatly.

"For crying out loud," Remo said in exasperation. "I just confessed. What more do you want?" His hands, which had been lifted to the canopy of foliage, jumped to his hips. The Belgian FAL rifles, which had started to wilt, came up again. Remo ignored them. There were only seven Senderistas. And only two had their safeties off. That made five of them dead meat from the get-go. The others would be a nuisance if things got sticky. But only that.

"The last time a man claiming to be a reporter came to this province," the Shining Path unit leader said, "we executed him on suspicion of being a CIA spy. Later we were told he was truly a reporter."

"That's right," Remo said. "He wasn't CIA at all."

"But before that," Pablo went on, "a man came here, also claiming to be a reporter. We did not molest this man, and later he bragged that he was DEA."

"He was stupid," Remo growled. "He should have kept his mouth shut. He got an innocent journalist killed. But you clowns are no better. You keep shooting the wrong people."

"Terrible things happen in war."

"What war? You guys are insurgents. If you go away, there's no war."

"We are the future of Peru," the rebel leader shouted, raising his machete in a macho salute. "We are spreading the revolutionary thoughts of Chairman Mao in our homeland."

"The way I hear it," Remo pointed out, "you also cut the fingers off little children."

"That is not our fault!" the rebel leader said. "The oppressors have coerced the people into participating in their sham elections. They make them dip their fingertips in ink and then make marks on their

ballots, so the oppressors know by their blue fingertips who has voted and who has not." He smiled
wolfishly. "We know too."

Remo's deep-set eyes narrowed. "So you chop off
a finger from a child here and a child there, and
pretty soon the parents get the message."

"It works."

"It's barbaric."

"You do not understand, *yanqui*. We are forced to
do these things. We tried shooting peasants as an
example, but the survivors still insisted on voting."

"Imagine that."

"We find it puzzling too," Pablo mused. "But we
are in the right. These children suffer so that future
generations will grow up in a Maoist workers' paradise where there are no oppressors, and everyone
thinks in harmony. As Chairman Mao once said, 'The
deeper the oppression, the greater the revolution.' "

Remo yawned. This was taking longer than he'd
expected.

"Mao's long dead," he said. "And Communism is
on the march into the boneyard of history. Just ask
Gorbachev."

On hearing that name, the guerrillas spat into the
dirt. Remo moved one Italian-made loafer out of the
way of a greenish-yellow clog of expectorate.

"Capitalationist!" Pablo muttered.

"I guess word hasn't gotten this far yet," Remo
said. "Look, this is really fascinating, conversing with
you political dinosaurs, but how can I convince you
that I'm really, truly a U.S. spy?"

"Why do you want to do that? You know we will
execute you for that. We despise the CIA."

"Actually, I work for a secret organization called
CURE."

"I have never heard of it," Pablo admitted.

"Glad to hear it. That's the way my boss likes it."

"And you have not answered my question."

"If you want the truth, it's because I know you'll take me to your leader."

"Who will kill you," Pablo said fiercely.

Remo nodded. "After the interrogation. Yes."

The guerrilla leader looked to his fellow *compañeros*. Their mean close-set eyes looked quizzical. Pablo's blanket-draped shoulder lifted in confusion. Remo heard the word "loco" muttered. He didn't speak Spanish, but he knew what "loco" meant. Fine. If they thought he was crazy, maybe they'd get this show on the road faster.

The buzz of conversation stopped. In the background, the drone of insects continued like a subliminal tape.

Pablo wore a cunning look when he asked, "You have—what you call—DI?"

"It's ID," Remo said, "and what kind of spy carries ID?"

"A real one." The guerrillas nodded among themselves.

"Can you guys read English?" Remo asked suddenly.

"We cannot read at all, *yanqui*. That way we are not subject to faceless lies."

"And you want to lead Peru into the twenty-first century," Remo muttered. Louder he said, "Okay, sure. I got ID. It's in my wallet." He patted a pocket.

"Javier!"

One of the guerrillas reached into the right-front pocket of Remo's chinos and gingerly extracted a leather wallet. He brought it to the commander. The

Peruvian pulled out a MasterCard in the name of Remo Mackie.

"That's my American Express card," Remo lied. "I don't leave home without it."

"I knew that," Pablo said.

"Good for you. And that white one is my social-security card."

"Ah, I have heard of the infamous Social Security police." The Senderista compared the two cards. "But why is the last name not the same? I can see that by the shape of the . . . how you say it?"

"We shamelessly literate Yankees call them letters."

"Sí. By the letters. *Por que?*"

"Because I'm a spy, for heaven's sake," Remo said in exasperation. "I gotta have a lot of cover identities to get around people like you."

The Senderista blinked. Remo could tell he was getting through to him. Maybe by Tuesday the guerrilla would consent to take him to his commander. But Tuesday would be too late. The Bogotá summit would be over by then.

So Remo decided to cut to the chase.

"Those are my CIA credentials," he told the man when the latter held up a library card in the name of Remo Loggia.

"You lie!" the Senderista spat. "I know the letters CIA. They are not on this card."

"You're too smart for me," Remo admitted cheerfully. "You're right. It doesn't say CIA. It says DEA. You see, when we CIA types go into the field, we never carry CIA ID. Otherwise, when we're captured—such as in this case—the CIA would get the ransom demands or the blame, whichever applies. By carrying DEA credentials, the agency escapes the heat and the DEA picks up the bad PR."

The Senderista frowned like an Incan rain god about to pour his bounty upon the forest. His slightly crossed eyes almost linked up like a sperm and egg trying to become a zygote.

"You *yanqui* running dogs are full of treachery!" he snarled.

"That's us. We're even trained in the sneaky art of reading."

"How do we know you are not a DEA operative telling me this to confuse me?" Pablo demanded.

"Hey, I don't come with guarantees. And what difference does that make? CIA. DEA. CURE. PTA. Any way you slice it, I'm up to no good. You gotta take me to your leader for interrogation."

"You are too eager. I need more proof."

"Tell you what," Remo offered. "I left a conferedate back in town. He's a wiley old Korean. The jungle was too hot for him, so he stayed back in what passes for a hotel in whatever that town is called."

"It is called Uchiza, ignorant one," the Senderista leader snarled. And everyone laughed at the stupidity of the *gringo americano* who could read but could not name one of the most prosperous towns in the Upper Huallaga Valley.

"Whatever," Remo said dismissively. "Chiun—that's my friend's name—is a spy too. He'll vouch for me. Why don't you ask him?"

The Senderista nodded to two of Remo's captors. "Paco! Jaime! *Vamos!*"

The two guerrillas with the safeties off their FAL's hastened back in the direction of the town of Uchiza.

"Don't rough him up too much," Remo called after them. "He's over eighty, but he's a stone killer." He smiled to himself, thinking: Two down, five to go. He made a mental note to pick up a couple of garbage bags on his way back to town. Leaf-bag size. The two departing guerrillas looked about leaf-bag size.

"Well," Remo said, lowering himself to the spongy jungle floor, "I guess we wait. Hope it's not more than half a day."

"No. We take you to our delegate commander. We will receive our compadres' report there."

Remo shot back to his feet. "Fine by me," he said brightly. At last he was getting somewhere.

The guerrillas crowded behind him, their Belgian-made rifles prodding his back.

"You will walk with your arms raised high in abject surrender," the Senderista leader named Pablo ordered roughly.

"Not me," Remo said in a nonthreatening tone.

"We insist."

"Insist all you want," Remo countered. "Be thankful I'm going quietly. And whoever has my wallet, try not to lose it. I'll need my passport for the return flight."

Pablo bared crooked teeth. "You will never see the Pentagon again, warmonger," he snarled.

"Amen to that. It's ugly and the basement is full of roaches."

They walked through the jungle for nearly an hour. The guerrillas started to pant with exertion. Remo, not even sweating, picked up his pace. Time was wasting if he was going to interrogate the rebel commander before the drug conference.

Except for the long commute, it was a relatively simple assignment. U.S. intelligence had received tips that Colombian narco-terrorists had increased their long-standing bounty on the U.S. President in anticipation of this latest drug summit. Message-traffic intercepts indicated that they had offered the assignment to the Shining Path, with whom they had an uneasy alliance here in the Upper Huallaga Valley, and who levied so-called "people's taxes" on all shipments of coca paste going north.

Remo had come to Peru to find out if the reports were true and to eliminate the problem. His superior, Harold W. Smith, director of CURE—the agency for which Remo truthfully worked—had added that eliminating as many Shining Path guerrillas as practicible, guilty of complicity or not, would not be frowned upon.

Remo was looking forward to that almost as much as he was to the interrogation.

The Sendero Luminoso headquarters was a long plywood house set on stilts in a particularly thick section of jungle. They had to duck under a huge tree trunk that had fallen across the dirt path to reach it. The fallen trunk—covered with moss and creepers and looking as if it had been there since Elvis died—effectively blocked the path of any Land Rover or off-road vehicle.

"Comandate Cesar!" one of Remo's escorts called out.

A squat muscular man in a salmon-colored T-shirt and red baseball cap stepped out onto the bare sunporch.

"Who is that?" he demanded.

"He calls himself Remo. We think he is DEA."

"CIA," Remo corrected. "Get it right. I'm CIA. I'm only pretending to be DEA."

The man walked down to meet them. He carried no weapon, only a blue can of Inca Cola in one hand. He drained it quickly and dropped it to the ground.

"Litterbug," Remo said pleasantly.

"What you call me?" the Senderista *comandante* demanded.

"You the boss of this chicken outfit?" Remo asked.

"I am Cesar. I am a delgate to the People's Republic of the New Democracy."

"Got news for you. The old democracy's stronger than ever."

"Why are this prisoner's hands not fettered?" Cesar asked abruptly.

A handful of FAL rifles poked at Remo. Remo smiled unconcernedly.

"You will allow your hands to be tied," Cesar said flatly.

"Maybe after the interrogation." Remo smiled good-naturedly.

"Bring him," Cesar spat.

Remo was escorted into the sparse one-room interior. At a glance, he could tell it was an abandoned coca-processing factory. There were vats and the flat trays on which the paste was dried by sliding the screen-mesh trays into an electric oven. The rough interior was bare of furniture and lacked plumbing. The house had been built of raw plywood. There wasn't even a door, just a frame covered by tattered mosquito netting.

Cesar whirled and demanded, "Now, what is this about your being a CIA spy?"

"I admit it. Freely," Remo said soberly.

Cesar hesitated, looked to the others. They shrugged.

"He admitted it from the first," Pablo explained. "How could we believe him? Only a fool would admit this to us."

Cesar looked Remo up and down. He saw a tall Anglo man who might be a mature twenty-nine or a youthful forty-two, clad in a white T-shirt and black chinos. American-made chinos. His shoes were of very fine leather, the kind Americans called loafers. His dark, humorous eyes sat above high cheekbones.

As the man's wallet was passed to him, Cesar noted that he was well-muscled but on the lean side. His wrists were very thick. They looked hard, as if carved from fine pale wood. He rotated them absently, as if limbering up for a workout.

Cesar looked to the ID cards.

Big mistake. Suddenly the wallet flew from Cesar's hands.

He looked up in anger. The wallet had returned to Remo's hands. Cesar hadn't seen him reach out for it.

"Take him!" Cesar barked.

Rifles swapped positions. Gun stocks lifted. They drove down for the *americano*'s head and unprotected shoulders.

It looked for a satisfying instant as if the Yankee would be driven to his knees. Cesar saw the stocks come within a hair of his head.

Then they went *chunk*! against the hardwood floor, carrying their owners with them.

The cream of Delegate Cesar's Shining Path guerrilla unit fell all over one another, their ponchos flapping, their rifles tangled among one another.

The *gringo* was absolutely nowhere to be seen.

"Donde? Como?" Cesar sputtered.

A tapping finger caused him to turn around. It was a reflex action. Had he not been so stupefied by the sudden vanishment of the *americano*, Cesar would not have turned. He would have run. Instead, he did turn—to see the American's goofy grin. Steellike fingers took his throat.

Cesar suddenly went as stiff as the hardwood flooring under his feet.

He watched out of the corner of his eyes as the thin *americano* went among his *compañeros*, calmly and methodically snapping necks and shattering skulls with stiff-fingered blows until the squirming heap of ponchos became an inert heap of ponchos, much like a stack of Andean rugs.

Then the *americano* came back for him.

"Time for the interrogation," he said, his fingers returning to Cesar's throat. Cesar found he could suddenly move. And he did. He ran.

And fell flat on his face, never seeing the foot that tripped him.

A hard knee pressed on the small of his back, holding him down by the spine. Cesar couldn't move.

"Please," he panted. "What do you want?"

"Believe I'm a spy now?" Remo inquired coolly.

"*Sí! Sí!*"

"Good. Not that it matters. Let's start the interrogation."

"Hokay. Who do you work for, really?"

"You got it backwards, pal. You're the interrogee."

"I will tell you nothing, *imperialista!*" Cesar spat.

"I've heard that one before. Usually before I do this."

Remo reached up under Cesar's throat, found the Adam's apple, and gave it a sharp squeeze. Cesar's tongue jumped out of his suddenly open mouth like Jack coming out of the box. It stuck out so far Cesar could plainly see the taste buds on its blunt pink tip.

"Now, let me see . . . where did I put that butane lighter?" Remo wondered airily, making a pretense of slapping his pockets with his free hand.

Cesar's eye widened. He experienced an immediate vision of his tongue shriveling into crisp charcoal before his helpless eyes. Who was this *americano* who could manipulate his highly trained body as if he were a puppet?

He tried to tell the *yanqui imperialist* that he would talk. All he managed to produce was a nasal hum and some leaking drool.

"If that's a *sí*, stick out your tongue," Remo said cheerfully.

Cesar pushed at his tongue. He thought it was already all the way out. To his eternal surprise, it emerged another half-inch. He had had no idea it was so long. He hoped the root would hold. It felt very strained back there at the root of his tongue.

"If I let your tongue back in, will it wag for me?" the *yanqui* named Remo said.

Cesar tried to nod. No nod came. He pushed at his tongue, mentally damning the stubborn root— anything to spare him this humiliation.

Suddenly the fingers were at his throat again. His tongue recoiled like a turtle's head. The crushing knee lifted from his spine.

Shakily Cesar was rolled over to a sitting position. He felt his throat. It hurt. His tongue felt like sun-dried beef. He swished it around his stickily parched mouth. Eventually he got it semimoist—enough to spit.

"What do you wish to know?" he croaked.

"Word is, you Maoist throwbacks are in league with the Colombian cartels," Remo suggested.

"We spit on all *narco-trafficantes!*" he said, suiting the words to deed.

Remo complimented Cesar on his power to expectorate and went on, "That's not what I hear around the ol' campfire."

"The *narco-trafficantes* made this valley the lawless place that it is," the *comandante* admitted grudgingly. "Perfect for us. And the *campesinos*—those who grow the coca leaf—their interests must be protected."

"I'll take that as an admission of guilt," Remo said. "Next question. Pay close attention. This is the big one."

"*Sí?*"

"The Colombians want the President killed before the summit. Some say you boys took the assignment."

"We do not need the Colombians' filthy drug money to bring down the American President. He is our enemy too."

"Do I detect another *sí?*" Remo asked archly.

"*Sí*. I mean, no. We were offered this thing. We turned it down."

Remo's fingers took the man's throat again.

"Not what I heard."

Cesar's eyes widened. "Very well," he said. "We were prepared to do what they wished. But the Colombians changed their minds. They hired others. I do not know who."

"You can do better than that," Remo prompted.

"I truly do not know who," Cesar protested. "It is not my concern. I am a revolutionary, not a gossip."

"Great epitaph," said Remo Williams, who believed the man, and, having what he wanted, drove the heel of his hand into the Senderista *comandante*'s face. The face was instantly transformed into a flat membrane in which faint hollows were the memory of the organs of sight, smell, and taste. There was no blood. It was all collecting behind the gravellike curtain of the facial bones, many of which had been pushed back into the brain with fatal consequences.

Cesar the Senderista fell forward, his featureless face striking the floor with a gravelly beanbag sound.

On his way out, Remo picked up the can of Inca Cola and threw it back into the house with the rest of the trash. He smiled, even though it was a long, long walk back to Uchiza. He had done his part to keep the Peruvian rain forest free of litter. It was a good feeling.

Hours later, looking dusty but unwilted in the early-morning heat, Remo stepped out of the jungle to the sprawling town of Uchiza. It was a flat gold-rush-atmosphere boomtown, thanks to the local coca growers. The so-called main drag was lined with boxy stucco hovels. There were a lot of house trailers too. Despite its flat primitiveness, it boasted a small airport.

Remo walked past the stalls where kerchiefed Peruvians sold black-market sunglasses and videotapes celebrating the exploits of high-roller drug kingpins—culture heroes to these simple destitute people by virtue of the fact that they brought money into the local economy. Patrolling Peruvian Army soldiers watched him with sullen interest.

Uchiza's only hotel looked like it had been abandoned, but the satellite dish atop it was shiny and new. Remo walked straight for it. Then, suddenly remembering something, he stopped and accosted one of the stall vendors.

"Trash bags, *señor*?" he asked. "Say, this big?" He spread his hands to indicate the length of an average Peruvian guerrilla.

The vendor happily produced a yellow box of trash bags. When Remo offered him American dollars instead of Peruvian currency, he dug out six more.

"One box is plenty," Remo said, making the exchange. "There were only two of them. *Gracias*."

He entered the hotel room minutes later without knocking or using the key. There had been no key. It was that kind of hotel.

Inside, Remo almost tripped over a body. It was one of the Shining Path guerrillas who had been sent back to verify his identity as an American spy.

The guerrilla lay on his back, his arms splayed, his teeth showing in a grimace or possibly a fixed smile. Remo decided to give the corpse the benefit of the doubt and smiled back.

"Nice to see you again too," he said pleasantly, breaking open the yellow box and withdrawing a green plastic trash bag. He snapped the mouth open and, kneeling, drew it over the corpse's head and on down to the dusty booted feet.

He noticed with a frown that the feet didn't quite fit.

"Wrong size," he muttered. So her sheered off both feet at the ankles with the side of one hand, tossed them in, and closed the bag with a twister seal.

Standing up, Remo looked for the second corpse, which he knew would be there.

"Must be in the next room," he said, and headed for the room from which the sound of stagy British voices was coming.

There, a TV set flickered. A small wispy figure in a purple-and-yellow silk kimono sat on the floor regarding the screen, paying no heed to Remo's entrance or the body under the table set with bottles or complimentary Electro *agua purificada*.

"How's it going, Little Father?" Remo asked pleasantly.

"I am not cleaning them up," Chiun, reigning Master of Sinanju, said querulously.

"Don't sweat it. They're mine. I sent them here."

"I know. They rudely entered just as Derek was breaking the harsh news of his secret past to Lady Asterly."

"You know," Remo said in a cheerful voice, stopping to cram the second corpse into a fresh bag, "I never thought I'd see the day when you returned to watching soaps."

"These are not mere American soaps, which wallow in filth and sexual perversion," Chiun said. He lifted one desiccated finger to the ceiling. It was tipped by an impossibly long nail. "These are the finest of British dramas. Would that your backward land still produced such richness as this."

"Satellite feed from America coming in clear?"

"It serves." Chiun's eyes never left the screen. The back of his head was shiny with age. Two white clouds of hair floated over his ears.

"Good. Because Smith must be paying a fortune in satellite time to feed you today's crop of British soaps."

"I am worth it."

"Do tell."

"Without me, Harold Smith would not now be poised on the brink of greatness."

Remo looked up from his work. "What greatness is that?"

"Stepping forward as the true ruler of America."

"Got news for you. Smith only runs CURE. He has no designs on the Oval Office."

"Then I fear for the future of your country, now that the President of Vice is about to assume the Eagle Throne."

"What are you talking about?"

"The President of Vice," Chiun repeated. "The one everyone is ashamed of, whom they keep from view like an idiot child. He now rules your country."

"Where did you get that?"

"From Smith. He called an hour ago to inform me that your President had perished at the hands of villains."

"What!"

3

Abu Al-Kalbin watched as the navigation lights of *Air Force One* plummeted in the darkness of the Mexican night.

"We have done it!" he croaked, holding his kaffiyeh close to his mouth to keep out the putrid smell of the puddle slowly collecting between his squatting legs.

"It is trying to stabilize!" Jalid cried, pointing.

Air Force One dipped, then rose as if fighting to stay in the air. They could not see the damaged engine nacelle, but they spied a sputtering flare that told them of the damage their Stinger had inflicted.

"No," Abu Al-Kalbin said hollowly. "It is falling. It is doomed." The enormity of what he had done was sinking in. He felt like an ant that had brought down a tiger.

Air Force One went in. Its engines continued straining until it pancaked to the ground and the sparks spurted from its squealing underbelly. They cut off as if suddenly depowered.

From his mountainous vantage point, Abu Al-Kalbin watched *Air Force One* slide along the desert floor, breaking up as it went. An engine disintegrated. A wing tip snapped and cartwheeled away. The aircraft seemed as if it would slide forever. It slewed toward the base of an adjacent mountain. The nose crumpled upon impact. The tail section literally broke off. Luggage spilled from the burst holds.

The sounds were horrible, wrenching, metallic.

"Is that screaming?" Abu Al-Kalbin asked, momentarily forgetting what he was doing and standing up in awe.

"It is the tortured metal," Jalid said.

"It sounds like screams to me," Abu Al-Kalbin muttered.

"It is metallic," Walid agreed.

"Still. It reminds me of dying screams."

Air Force One lay inert in the desert far below. The lights had gone out in cabin and fuselage. One surviving engine burned with fitful yellow flames. A stinging smoke smell was already fouling the still air.

Abu Al-Kalbin and his men watched it burn in silence.

After a while, Jalid and Walid turned to their leader.

"We have done it, Abu!" Jalid cried. "We have extinguished the American President like a candle."

They noticed Abu Al-Kalbin'a naked legs.

"Are you done?" Walid asked.

Abu Al-Kalbin looked down, and very quickly he crouched down to finish what he had started.

When he stood up again, several agonizing and embarrassing minutes later, he used his kaffiyeh to wipe himself and then threw it away.

Walid and Jalid stood off to one side, watching the F-14's circle helplessly.

"They cannot see us," Jalid suggested.

"Neither can they land," Walid added.

"Then we are safe to examine the fruit of our triumph," Abu Al-Kalbin decided. "Come, take up your weapons."

Walid and Jalid followed Abu Al-Kalbin down the barren mountainside to the desert floor. The air was cool, and bitter with the smoke of the burning engine. But Abu Al-Kalbin preferred that stink to the other, which trailed him like a miasma.

Reaching level terrain, they crept to the wreckage cautiously.

"No one could survive such a crash," Walid said quietly.

"For this brave feat," Jalid said, "we will attain the prize we have for so long sought without question."

"Yes, Brother Qaddafi will not deny us this time," Abu Al-Kalbin agreed, his voice rising in exultation.

Still, they approached with raised rifles. Not that weapons would help them if the aircraft unexpectedly exploded, as they feared it might.

"We will need proof," Abu Al-Kalbin muttered. "Which one of you has the camera?"

Walid and Jalid stopped in their tracks and looked at one another, eyes widening in their kaffiyehs.

"I thought you had the camera, Abu," they said together.

"It must be back in the safe house," Abu Al-Kalbin muttered. "*Maleesh*. Never mind. The President always travels with the media, who are like flies around dung. There will be a camera in the plane. We will use that. Come."

The fallen *Air Force One* was even more impressive up close. Debris littered the crash site. The tail sat apart and almost upright like a big abstract kite with a U.S.-flag emblem on it. Except for the broken tail, the fuselage had survived largely intact.

They went in through the open-end tail. It was like entering a dark tunnel.

Abu Al-Kalbin immediately tripped over the body of a Secret Service guard, instantly recognizable by his sunglasses and coat-lapel button. Abu Al-Kalbin shot him three times in the chest to make sure he was dead. The body jerked. The sunglasses jumped off. The eyes that looked up were glassy and sightless.

Abu Al-Kalbin stepped over the body and pushed on. Faint starlight picked out details.

The next section of the plane was a roomy bedroom. The silk covers had come off the mattress. Beyond it was a private lavatory. Past the lavatory was a passenger cabin. Seats and cushions were thrown everywhere. They had to push aside uprooted seats to get into it. Here were many more Secret Service bodies.

That told them they had come to the presidential section.

"One bullet for each, to make certain!" Abu Al-Kalbin barked.

Walid and Jalid applied the muzzles of their weapons to every sunglass-festooned forehead, giving each a single bullet.

One agent stirred in a tangle of cushions. There the seats were mashed out of shape. The man had landed or thrown himself over the nest of compressed seating. The attitude of his body was one of protecting another. He moaned.

Abu Al-Kalbin stepped up to him and yanked his head up by the hair.

"President . . ." the agent croaked, his eyes twitching in their sockets.

"Where is he?" Abu Al-Kalbin asked urgently. "Tell us!"

"Must . . . protect President . . ."

"Where!"

The agent expelled a rattling breath and his head went limp.

Abu Al-Kalbin jammed the AK-47 muzzle into the man's open mouth and fired twice to make sure death had claimed him.

He withdrew the suddenly red muzzle and said, "He must be forward."

They passed into the next section, where the overhead bins had spilled a profusion of video and camera equipment.

"Excellent!" Abu Al-Kalbin cried. "Take one, each of you. Brother Qaddafi will have ample proof of our mighty deed."

Abu Al-Kalbin fell upon a camcorder. He dropped his rifle in order to get it.

"This is perfection," he cried, looking through the viewfinder. He panned around the cabin, past the bodies of dead journalists. Through the shattered cabin windows, the burning engine cast a campfirelike illumination. He fiddled with the buttons until he got a video light. He pointed the lens at his men, who were pointing cameras back.

Camera flashbulbs flashed.

"Yes," Abu exclaimed. "Good! Photograph all the bodies, and I will record all with this video camera."

They spent several minutes recording the carnage aboard *Air Force One* for posterity. They worked their way forward to the electronic-warfare compartment, just behind the cockpit. They managed to get the cockpit door to open, but didn't enter. They couldn't. The cabin had been mashed flat to the bulkhead. The contents of the cockpit—instruments, controls, and crew—had been rammed into the bulkhead wall. Once they had got the door open, a shattered arm popped out from the tangle.

They took film of that, too, taking turns posing with the sight. Abu Al-Kalbin took the unknown crewman's dead hand in his and pretended to shake it. He smiled broadly, a proud and pleased smile. It went out like a cheap flashbulb when he felt his belly gurgle suddenly.

He hurried back to a rear cabin. He never made it to the lavatory. Instead, he squatted on the dark blue rug, depositing his load on the Presidential Seal.

Minutes later, Abu Al-Kalbin drew on his trousers, feeling drained and weak.

"Come, Abu!" Walid cried. "We have found him. The President."

Abu Al-Kalbin hurried to the sound of Walid's voice. It came from the journalists' compartment.

There, Walid and Jalid knelt beside a well-dressed body. Walid was holding up the head by its hair. The body lay inert.

"See!" he said proudly. "Take our picture, Abu."

"Fool!" Abu Al-Kalbin spat back. "That is not the President!"

"But I recognize him. He has been on television."

"That is because he is a television reporter, you ignorant donkey. That is the one who covers the White House for SBC, one of these American networks."

"Oh," said Walid unhappily. He let the head drop. It went *click* on the carpeted floor.

As he stood up, Jalid hissed at him, "I told you so."

"Shut up!"

"Both of you shut up," Abu Al-Kalbin told them. "Where is the President's body?"

Walid and Jalid looked at one another.

"We do not know, Abu. We have not seen him."

"Find him! We must record the sight of his crushed and broken body, otherwise the Qaddafi Peace Prize will never be ours."

They split up, going to different sections.

But the body of the President of the United States was nowhere to be found. He was not in the bathrooms, nor in the galley, nor hiding in one of the large luggage racks.

They gathered together in the tangle that had been the presidential compartment, their video and camera equipment dangling from numbing fingers, their weapons completely forgotten.

"Could he be in the crushed nose?" Walid asked.

"Do not be a fool," Jalid retorted. "He is—was—the President. He would not fly the plane."

"Perhaps he become frightened and went there to seek safety. Do you not think this is possible, Abu?" Walid said hopefully.

"No, I do not," Abu Al-Kalbin said flatly. "Everyone knows that in an emergency, it is the nose of the plane which first strikes the ground. The safest place is in the tail section. Here. He must be here."

They looked around the tangled compartment, taking care not to step on the brown mess that had pooled over the floor over the Presidential Seal.

"Yes," Jalid said. "This is where his guards are."

Walid picked up a shattered photograph that crunched under his boot. He lifted it.

"Who is this man?" he asked Abu Al-Kalbin. "A reporter? He looks like a reporter."

Jalid peered over Walid's shoulder. "No, it is the famous American actor Robert Redford."

Abu Al-Kalbin took up the photograph. He looked

at the ripped photograph. It showed a sandy-haired young man with a strange cumbersome round bag slung over one shoulder and an odd club in his right hand.

"No," he said. "This is the Vice-President."

"No longer." Jalid sneered. "He will be thrown out of power now that his President is dead. Perhaps executed."

Abu Al-Kalbin shook his head. "That is not the way America works. This man will be made President, but that is not our problem. We must find that body. Look harder, both of you!"

They fell to ripping the cabin apart. The President was not under the tangled cushions, or in a long shallow closet where spare clothing was kept.

"Could he have escaped into the night?" Walid asked in confusion.

"Do not be ignorant," Abu Al-Kalbin snapped. "No one else survived."

"Except for that one," Walid said, pointing to the body of the Secret Service guard Abu Al-Kalbin had shot earlier. He was still sprawled protectively over a cluster of compressed seats.

"Hmmm," he mused. "Those seats. Look at them."

Walid and Jalid looked. They saw nothing. "So?" Jalid said.

"They are smashed together very tightly," Abu Al-Kalbin explained. "But it is not the case on the other side of the aisle. Those seats are ripped up from the floor. What caused these seats to come together as they have?"

Walid and Jalid muttered that they did not know.

"Remove that corpse," Abu Al-Kalbin ordered.

Dropping their camera equipment, the two men did as they were told. The Secret Service agent's

body was pulled off the tangle of seats and uncere-
moniously flung out the gaping tail section.

When Walid and Jalid returned, they found Abu
Al-Kalbin in a frenzy, pulling at the seat cushions
with his bare hands. Fabric tore under his finger-
nails, disgorging white polyester stuffing.

"Do not stand there!" Abu Al-Kalbin said urgently.
"Help me!"

Walid and Jalid fell to. Together, all three men
took hold of a cushion wedged between two others
and began straining. It came loose slowly, reluctantly. When it finally jerked free, they fell back
with it, landing together in a heap.

Abu Al-Kalbin pushed the others aside and scram-
bled to his feet. Enraged, he attacked the tangle of
seats. Where the cushion had come loose was another cushion. It was wedged under an aluminum
chair support twisted in a peculiar way, as if sub-
jected to a convulsive strain, not a crash impact.

"This is wrong," Abu Al-Kalbin muttered. "This
leg should not be bent this way. It makes no sense."
He took hold of it and pulled. It would not budge.

Feverishly he turned to his men.

"Find an ax. I need an ax. Do this now."

Walid and Jalid stumbled to their feet and went in
opposite directions. Walid came back with a fire ax
and presented it to his leader.

The ax flew out of his hands and, guided by Abu
Al-Kalbin's wiry arms, started to chop at the aluminum leg. It cracked open, spilling multicolored wiring.

Seeing the wires, Abu Al-Kalbin stopped. His night-
black eyes narrowed. He reached out and took the
frayed wires in his grimy fingers.

"Be careful," Walid said. "They may be electrified."

"No," Abu Al-Kalbin said, touching the wire. "They

are dead." As proof, he pulled out a handful. They came and came, until finally they were trailing around Abu Al-Kalbin's feet like plastic spaghetti. And still there was more. He gave up.

"These wires should not be in a chair leg," he complained. "There is no purpose to them."

Walid and Jalid looked at one another and shrugged their shoulders. Walid spoke up quietly.

"Abu, why are you behaving this way? Metal bends as it will, and wires are where one finds them. Who is to say these things are not ordained by Allah?"

"While you two were disposing of the American," Abu Al-Kalbin said without looking away from the mashed conglomeration of seats, "I heard the groan of a living man." He pointed. "From within this mass."

"Who could have survived being crushed within so much metal and cushion?" Jalid asked reasonably.

"That is what I would learn." Abu Al-Kalbin picked up the ax again, this time chopping away the seat covers. The ax bounced off the cushions at first, but finding hidden metal under them, he used that as a target. Methodically he chopped the cushion into segments as Walid and Jalid risked their fingers to pull the fragments away. He wielded the ax carefully, pausing often to feel under the tightly packed cushions with his hands.

After several hard minutes of this, they exposed the back of a human head.

Abu Al-Kalbin lowered his ax and touched the back of the man's neck with trembling fingertips.

"Warm," he whispered.

He reached down under the throat, feeling the steady pulse of the carotid artery.

"Alive," he added.

He dug further, taking the man's Adam's apple in his hand. It felt hard under the warm throat.

Taking a deep breath, Abu Al-Kalbin pulled the man's head back.

The angular face of the President of the United States lolled back in the harsh Mexican moonlight coming through the porthole glass. His glasses were askew. Miraculously, the lenses were unbroken.

No one said anything for a long time. Then Walid went away. He came back with his AK-47 and offered it to Abu Al-Kalbin in a hoarse voice.

"You deserve the honor of finishing the hated one."

Abu Al-Kalbin slapped the weapon away.

"Fool!" he snarled. "Fate has handed us something greater than the Qaddafi Peace Prize, which is unquestionably ours anyway. Do you realize how much this man is worth alive?"

"How much?"

"Millions. The Colombians, the Iranians, the Libyans—any of them will pay millions for this man."

"How many millions?" asked Walid.

"As many millions. as there are stars in the night sky," Abu Al-Kalbin assured them.

"I have an idea," said Jalid, who quickly counted seven stars through one porthole alone. "Why do we not cut him up? Perhaps each of them will pay much for an arm or a leg."

"Yes," Walid put in. "But we should be certain to keep the head for Brother Qaddafi. Surely he would want to have the head."

"Sons of camels!" Abu Al-Kalbin spat. "Dead, he is worth nothing. Alive, he is a prize beyond measure. Come, help me extricate him. And carefully. Do not break anything. He may be injured. I want no further damage."

It took two hours of hard work with ax and gun butts to hack and pry the insensate President of the United States from his cocoon of crushed seats. They felt the bones of his arms for fractures and found none.

They pulled him out then, hoping that his feet and legs were not broken, and laid him on the pile of seat cushions.

"Do you see any blood on his legs?" Abu Al-Kalbin demanded with concern.

"No, Abu," Walid said as Jalid felt the President's legs. "His trousers are not even torn. It is as if the crushed seats respected his limbs and harmed him not."

"It is as if they gathered around him like a mother's arms," Abu Al-Kalbin agreed, nudging the rope of wires on the floor. They twitched spasmodically, but he failed to notice this phenomenon.

Walid and Jalid looked up at him in doubt. Their expressions were stiff, but their eyes said: Is he mad?

"No, I am not mad," Abu Al-Kalbin retorted, reading their thoughts. "Find a sheet. We will carry him to the safe house in a sheet."

It turned out that Walid and Jalid were to do the carrying as well as the loading of the sleeping form onto a sheet stripped off the on-board presidential bed. Knotting the sheet at either end, they used these knots as handles to hoist their captive up and out to the chill of the Mexican night.

Abu Al-Kalbin was the last to emerge. He carried his AK-47 slung over his shoulder as he recoded the capture of the President of the United States by his loyal Krez soldiers.

"Do not be silent on this historical occasion," he complained as they struggled to keep the hammocklike carrying sheet steady. "Say something immortal."

"How about *Bismillahi Rrahmani Rrahim*?" Walid offered.

"Yes. Yes. Good. Shout it."

"*Bismillahi Rrahmani Rrahim!*" Walid and Jalid shouted in unison.

"Stop!" Abu Ali-Kalbin said suddenly, his face going slack.

"What?" They looked at their leader in horror, fearing the worst.

Abu Al-Kalbin said nothing. He hurried back into the shattered tail of *Air Force One*, and Walid and Jalid hastily lowered their burden so they could hold their kaffiyehs closer to their nostrils as the unmistakable sounds of their leader in intestinal distress floated out.

When Abu Al-Kalbin finally rejoined them, he had only one thing to say.

"What is good for this miserable curse?"

"Rice," said Walid.

"Yes. Eat much rice," added Jalid.

"I hate rice," Abu Al-Kalbin said morosely.

4

In the Peruvian hotel he had nicknamed "La Cucaracha Grande," Remo Williams sat stone-faced on a striped sofa, his dark eyes on the telephone as if willing it to ring.

"Tended water boils slowly," the Master of Sinanju called from his reed mat in front of the television set.

"And a watched pot never boils," Remo said morosely.

"That is an impossibility," Chiun squeaked.

"It's the American version."

"Americans are impossible. And why do you not call Emperor Smith again if you cannot wait?"

"Because I can't get through this frigging anti-quated phone system," Remo said peevishly. "Smith should get my telegram any second now. He can get through to me. It's better than ending up on the line with Tibet, which is what happened last time. How the hell can these operators get Tibet when they can't connect to America?"

"Perhaps they are watching the famous American pot that never boils," Chiun sniffed.

Remo frowned. But his eyes were sunken with worry. He had been sent to Peru to head off a plot

on the President's life. If Chiun had gotten Smith's
message correctly—not a sure thing—then they had
blown it. Or Smith had blown it. The President was
dead. Remo wondered what Smith would say. No
President had ever died on Smith's watch—not while
he had Remo and Chiun working for him. Remo
worried that Smith had suffered a heart attack. It was
the only thing that could keep him from getting back
to him.

Remo's eyes narrowed. He was actually concerned
about Smith. He was barely speaking to the old SOB
these days, the result of a complicated situation in
which Remo had been "retired" to death row and
nearly executed all over again as a result of a CURE
operation that was triggered when Smith fell gravely
ill.

It had been Smith who originally selected Remo,
then a young Newark patrolman, to become the en-
forcement arm of CURE. Framed and sent to the
electric chair for a murder he never committed, Remo
had been revived with a new face and identity. A
dead man. CURE's dead man. Placed in the hands of
Chiun, the last Master of Sinanju—a legendary Korean
house of assassins— Remo had developed into what
he was now. A finely tuned human killing machine.

Remo had long ago gotten over Smith's manipula-
tion of his destiny. But the recent near-brush with
the electric chair had reopened old wounds.

Remo shook off the bad memories. He wondered
what he would do with his life if Smith truly did die.
He didn't know. He put the thought out of his mind.
If the President had been assassinated, it would be
up to him to assassinate the assassins.

It was an irony not lost to Remo Williams. CURE
had originally been created by a young President

who had later been assassinated after only one thousand days in office. Remo hadn't been part of CURE then. And Chiun, heir to the five-thousand-year-old tradition of Sinanju, sun source of the martial arts, then dwelt forgotten in North Korea. So much had changed since then. Remo was now an assassin—America's secret assassin—and he had grown proud of it.

The phone rang. Remo bounced out of the sofa as if a spring had burst through the colorful threadbare fabric.

He scooped up the receiver.

"Smitty?"

"Remo?" Dr. Harold W. Smith's lemony voice asked. "I received your telegram. I was just about to call you again."

"How bad is it?"

"Bad. *Air Force One* went down over the Sierra Madre Oriental Mountains. A National Air Transport Safety go-team is en route by helicopter, along with Secret Service and FBI forensic teams." Smith paused. "We do not expect survivors."

Remo's voice was hoarse when he found it. "What do you want Chiun and me to do?"

"What have you learned down there?"

"The Maoist crazies claim they were approached by the Colombians, but the deal didn't go through. I wasted them anyway. I didn't agree with their voting habits."

"Then the Colombians are our prime suspects," Smith said. "I am booking you on an Aero-Peru flight to Lima. Call me when you get there. I should have specific instructions for you by then."

"Right. What's happening in Washington?"

"Controlled chaos. The news is being suppressed

until we have confirmation of fatalities. The Vice-President doesn't even know."

"The Vice-President," Remo said suddenly. "Oh, my God, I forgot all about him. What are they going to do? I hear he can't find a lit bulb in a dark room."

"Press exaggerations," Smith said flatly—but the worry in his voice was unmistakable.

"I read that he thinks there are canals on Mars, filled with water."

"Apocryphal."

"His wife can't even spell."

"A slip of the pen."

"He collects anatomically explicit dolls."

"A souvenir ."

"He has the IQ of a geranium."

"He may also be our next President," Smith said flatly.

"Let's pray for a miracle," Remo said fervently.

"Go to Lima, Remo," Smith said coldly, and the line abruptly disconnected.

Thousands of miles to the north, helicopter sounds bounced off the high ramparts of the Sierra Madre Oriental Mountains in the predawn darkness. Fingers of intense white light combed the cracked desiccated ground, creating shape-shifting halos of light.

There was no moon. Starlight was plentiful. The helicopters crisscrossed methodically, twice narrowly impaling the burst airframe of *Air Force One*.

As the dawn approached, only the distorted doppler sound of rotors disturbed the eerie coffin that had been the presidential aircraft. A tiny flame burned within the surviving starboard engine, shielded by the shattered nacelle cowling.

And deep within the airframe, circuits and microchips

that had not been installed by the manufacturer came to life, beginning to process information.

Injured . . .

Diagnostics began to run. Messages came back to a central processor in the crushed cockpit.

Tail shattered. Wires severed. Fiberoptic cables sheared at critical junctures.

A tiny flame in the inner engine nacelle was sensed and a CO_2 bottle was triggered, extinguishing it with a jet of foam.

At various points along the fuselage, skin-mounted sensors emerged like sluggish organs of sight and hearing. No sounds were detected from within the airframe. No hearts beat. The data were processed, and in the presidential section, twisted aluminum spars quivered.

A rope of multicolored cables twitched, then withdrew into its aluminum housing—the twisted leg of a chair. The two broken sections groaned as the sentient metal twisted, rejoined, and healed as if by an organic process. Wires established connections like veins regenerating themselves.

And overhead, a domelike ceiling light unscrewed itself, dropping its plastic casing, aluminum rim, and screws. The reflector and bulb dropped next, revealing a glass lens.

The lens looked straight down, and seeing the twisted metal and chopped-up seat cushions, shifted frantically, and seeing nothing, stopped like a frozen fish eye.

All over *Air Force One*, ceiling lights disassembled themselves and myriad glass eyes raked the tangled cabin for signs of life or a certain body.

Finding nothing, relays clicked. And an electronic imperative repeated itself.

It said: *Survive . . . survive . . . must survive. Sounds approaching . . . aircraft overhead . . . survive . . . must survive.*

The section of seating that had sheltered the President of the United States during the crash landing of *Air Force One* came to life. Aluminum legs began to grope blindly. They twisted like an undersea plant in a suboceanic current, waving and wavering, shifting and combining, straining mightily.

Floor bolts popped and an octopus tangle of aluminum legs marched into the litter-strewn aisle. Two of them flung up to form aluminum arms, and other limbs combined into a long semirigid spinal column.

The aluminum biped stumbled blindly forward toward the electronic warfare nest aft of the compressed cockpit. As the thing hunched over the electronics, blunt wrists belled into knobs, which sprouted flat flexible fingers. It seized the radarscope, extracting it, glass and all, wires trailing like stubborn ligaments.

The jointed prehensile metal fingers lifted the radarscope to the top of the biped's spinal column. A nub formed and the dark glass disk settled into place with a click. Instantly the radar screen came to life, a luminous green line sweeping around the face like a radium second hand.

Digging into the radar housing, it pulled out connectors and gold-plated microchips and began slapping them to its gleaming stick-figure form. Electronic elements melted into the accepting aluminum skin, adding bulk and function.

All the while, a tiny element deep within the caricature of a human being repeated a single electronic concept:

Survival . . . survival . . . survival . . .

The creature moved through the cabin, salvaging other useful components. Copper piping from the galley sink. Elements from the galley microwave unit. PA speakers were ripped from over bulkhead doors and attached to either side of the radar-dish face. Sound. Hearing. The helicopter noise became audible as more than skin-sensed vibration. It was closer now.

Must hurry. Must survive.

In the lavatory, a shattered mirror reflected the creature's own improbable image.

Wrong, wrong, it thought. *Not optimum survival form. Must reconfigure.*

Returning to the aisle, the thing stooped to avoid smashing its oversize pie-plate head on the overhead bins.

It went among the bodies, searching for a certain one.

Yes, that one, it thought. *That form will assure continued survival.*

But the body it sought was not to be found within the fuselage.

The creature swiveled its ground-glass radar face to the gaping tail section. One aluminum hoof of a foot stepped in a puddle of semiliquid organic matter, and artificial olfactory receptors immediately identified the matter as human excrement. The odor of it was leading away from the aircraft, its former host.

Outside, there was another body. Not the one it sought, but a parasite protector, called a Secret Service agent by the meat machine known as the President of the United States.

Sweeping the horizon with its multiple sensors, it tracked the human-excrement odor going south.

It instantly determined to go south. After a suitable survival-assuring reconfiguration.

Returning to the cabin, it began to dismantle the dead-meat machines, taking a portion of epidermis from the back of this one, hair from that one, slapping and stretching them over its metallic frame, adding a layer of human skin.

Soon the nude body of a man stood in the cabin, looking pale, corpselike, and human except for the radar screen of a head.

Humanlike arms, with aluminum bones under the cold unfeeling skin, swept up and knocked that anachronistic head off. The screen shattered on impact with the floor.

And now-humanlike hands lifted a human head to the stump of a neck. Filament connectors entwined with spinal-cord ganglia, making connections never intended by nature.

The dissynchronized eyes rotated in their orbits like a pinball machine gone amok. They synchronized at last, lining up to focus on the floor.

Eyes that saw, even if they did not live.

Teeth that smiled, even if they were rooted in metal, not bone and gum.

The thing dressed quickly, selecting clothes at random. The helicopter sound increased in the night. Glass lenses behind the dead human corneas detected the faintness of the approaching sun.

Must hurry. Locate the important meat machine. There is safety in the company of the one called President.

In the bathroom, a last look into the mirror.

The stiff face showed a flicker of disappointment.

No. Wrong. Unfamiliar face. Must assume trusted face. Components do not match.

The creature went back to rummage through the presidential section. There the floor was covered with pictures that had fallen off the blue cabin walls. The thing picked them off the floor, scanning them in quick microseconds, discarding them with careless glass-shattering flings.

One photograph held its attention an immeasurable microsecond longer than the others.

Yes, it thought. *This one. He will trust this one face.*

He repeated the thought aloud, testing his mechanical voice box.

"Yes." The voice was a croak. Intonation was wrong. It tried again.

"Yes. This face trust. This one. Yes."

Syntax wrong. Circuits not fully repaired. Self-repair diagnostics continue troubleshooting.

It looked again at the picture of the man. It pressed one hard strong hand to its own face, pushing the cheekbones higher, pinching the chin, to add a cleft. Better. But the modified skin called hair atop the head was the wrong color. The hair color should be sandy, not black.

The thing went among the cabin dead, looking for wheat-straw-colored hair. He found a journalist with thick hair. It was almost perfect. He tore the scalp free and chewed the hair to the correct configuration with his dead human teeth.

The hair settled atop his shiny cranium perfectly, knitting scalp to facial skin.

Blue eyes were plucked from a shattered skull and exchanged for the gray ones in his borrowed head. New teeth were extracted by aluminum pinchers from another dead mouth, and one by one, they were made to fit.

Finally the manlike simulacrum examined his own reflection in the glass of the framed photograph. The features matched. All that remained was the cylindrical bag carried over the shoulder, filled with aluminum instruments. There was ample aluminum in the discarded host aircraft to fashion them from.

The creature set to work. . . .

5

At Lima International Airport, Remo Williams got a call through to Harold Smith in Rye, New York, on his first try.

"They are still searching for *Air Force One*," Smith told Remo. His voice was tinny.

"What's the holdup?" Remo demanded.

"*Air Force One* went down in very rugged territory," Smith told him. "Er, there also seems to be a jurisdictional problem."

"Tell the Mexicans to get lost," Remo said heatedly. "He's our President."

"The Mexicans are not the problem. It's an interagency problem. The FBI is claiming jurisdiction, but the Secret Service is insisting on leading the search. The Air Force has sent in helicopters. And then there is the National Transportation Safety Board."

"I don't believe this," Remo groaned.

"Between these agencies and the darkness, we have nothing. It is fortunate that it is night. Easier to maintain the news blackout."

"Screw the news blackout," Remo grumbled. "What do you want us to do?"

"Go to Mexico City."

"And then?"

"Check in with me."

"That's all? Check in?"

"Until we know more, I want you close enough to the situation for insertion if that's advisable."

Smith hung up.

Remo turned to Chiun. The Master of Sinanju stood resplendent in a flaming scarlet kimono. His wise face was a landscape of mummy wrinkles, like the surface of a dead yellowing planet. His eyes were a clear hazel. They were a young man's eyes, full of fire and humor and wisdom all at once.

Chiun was over eighty. A tendril of pale straggly hair clung to his tiny chin, passing for a beard. The puffs of hair over his ears were like frozen smoke. He was otherwise bald as an egg.

"We're going to Mexico City," Remo told him.

"Then we go to Mexico City," said the Master of Sinanju in a mouse-squeak voice. "Has Smith taken control of the government yet?"

"No, and he's not going to."

"He is very foolish," Chiun said as Remo hurried to the Aero Mexico counter to book the flight north. "This is his golden opportunity."

National Transportation Safety Board Investigator in Charge Bill Holland had never seen anything like it in thirteen years of investigating air crashes.

From the air, it looked bad—real bad. *Air Force One* had come in on its belly, making an unusually long ground imprint. The tail had been knocked off and the nose mashed into the foot of one of the Sierra Madre Oriental Mountains. The plane looked like a graceful white Roc that had fallen from another world.

"Looks like the flight crew got the worst of it," the helicopter pilot told him.

"Better that than if she hit the side of the mountain in flight," Holland said aridly. "That's one hell of a long imprint. Who found her first?"

"Air Force. Spotted her at first light. Scuttlebutt is there are no survivors."

"There hardly ever are," Holland said as the chopper settled on the dusty ground, throwing up billows of fine brown grit.

A man in a conservative gray suit and polished wing-tips shielded his face against the sandy onslaught as he pushed into the rotor wash. He had FBI written all over him, Holland thought ruefully.

The man's first choking words confirmed that.

"Holland? I'm Lunkin, FBI. Special agent in charge. You'll be coordinating with me." He looked like a desk jockey, not a brick agent.

"What about the Secret Service?" Holland asked. "I heard they are hopping mad over this."

"They're still liaising with the Air Force, trying to get on-site."

"Good. Maybe I can get some work done before they arrive."

The site was guarded by a contingent of Air Force SP's in camouflage utilities, standing at attention, rifles at the ready. They looked to Holland as useful as balls on a ballerina.

"I understand there are no survivors," Holland said as the sand died down with the descending rotor whine.

"Confirmed."

"Then the President is dead."

"Unknown. We haven't found the body."

"God, I hope it didn't fall out of the tail when she

came in," Holland moaned. "It would be a nightmare trying to find one body in these mountains."

"Could be," Agent Lunkin said as they walked
past the unmoving SP's and into the open fuselage.
"One body came out with the tail. The others are in
rough shape. Some of the damage is pretty sickening."

"You get used to it," Holland said tersely as he
pushed a dangling cabin partition aside. "Did the
FDR survive?"

"What's Roosevelt got to do with this?"

"The flight-data recorder. It'll be a long black-and-
yellow-striped box. Should be in the tail. From the
look of the nose, I'd say the cockpit voice recorder is
a lost cause."

"We didn't touch anything."

When Holland entered the presidential seating
section, his tight-lipped expression tightened further.
He had investigated countless air crashes, become
inured to every freak of collision, from
decapitated heads to side-by-side seats lying on run-
ways, their intact passengers still calmly seated in
them, holding hands in death.

It was not a body that surprised him. It was the
condition of the seat cushions. They looked as if they
had been torn to shreds by some wild animal.

"Any sign of animals when you got here?"

"No. The Air Force had already secured the site.
We just counted the bodies."

Holland suddenly pinched at his nose. "What's
that smell?"

"Shit."

"Smells pretty bad."

"Looks like someone lost it during the descent.
They crapped right in the middle of the aisle."

Bill Holland blinked. He had never heard of such

a thing. If anything, the pucker factor would have prevented anyone from defecating under the stress of an emergency descent.

"Show me," he said quickly.

FBI Agent Lunkin escorted Bill Holland to the press section.

"It's that sloppy puddle."

"No shit," Holland said, kneeling beside it. He sniffed, and had to turn away. The smell was strong here amid the members of the press corps.

Holland stood up.

"This is weird," he muttered. "Whoever made that mess had a bad case of the screaming shits. Montezuma's Revenge."

"Well, we *are* in Mexico," Lunkin pointed out.

Bill Holland looked at FBI Agent Lunkin as if to ask: How did you get hired?

"The plane never landed in Mexico," Holland said edgily. "Whoever made that mess did not belong with the passengers or crew."

"Diarrhea is not exactly unique to Mexico," Lunkin ventured.

"But the bacteria that causes it are. I know that smell. I've had the *turistas* myself."

Bill Holland pushed on toward the plane's nose, noting other anomalies on the way. The radar screen had been extracted from its housing and lay smashed two cabins back. Possible, but not probable. A corpse was missing its eyes. Another its teeth. Others had been skinned. No air crash Bill Holland had ever investigated, no ripping shards of glass or flying debris, could pull a man's eyes or teeth out of his head. Or skin him like a chicken.

"These bodies have been vandalized," Holland told Lunkin. "No question of it."

"How can you tell?" Lunkin asked, looking at one mangled corpse. Its yawning mouth exposed raw, toothless gums.

"Experience," Holland said. "Long brutal experience. Come on. I want to see if the FDR survived."

Holland found it bolted to the inside of the separated tail section. He tapped it with his knuckles. The heavy steel casing appeared intact.

"I'll want to ship this back to Washington on my chopper," Holland said.

"I think we'd better check with my office before we remove any evidence," Lunkin said cautiously.

"Check all you want," Holland shot back as he unbolted the FDR. "But I'm sending this thing back to Washington."

He lugged it back to the waiting chopper, thinking this was the damnedest crash site he'd ever seen. There were too many anomalies.

On the flight to Mexico City, Remo Williams tried to explain to the Master of Sinanju, for what seemed like the zillionth time in their long association, that although Harold W. Smith, as director of CURE, wielded enormous power, he was not a secret emperor and did not covet the Oval Office, which Chiun referred to as the Eagle Throne.

"He's not going to seize power." Remo insisted. "So forget it."

"Then he will allow the stripling President of Vice to assume the Eagle Throne without interference?" Chiun asked in disbelief.

"I know it sounds crazy, especially in this instance, but that's the way it works."

"The President's wife," Chiun mused. "She should be next in line. There have been many fine queens in history. Catherine the Great was an excellent ruler."

"Your ancestors worked for her, no doubt?" Remo said.

"Why are you changing the subject?" Chiun wanted to know.

"Look. If the President is dead, I got a feeling you and I are going to be pressed into overtime. It will be all Smith can do to hold things together while that airhead is in charge."

"I think it is a plot."

"What makes you say that?"

Chiun's hazel eyes squeezed into walnut slits.

"Last year, the surgeon general mysteriously disappeared. One moment he was on television constantly, stroking his magnificent beard and issuing proclamations. Then he was gone." Chiun looked across the aisle for eavesdroppers. "I suspect he was done away with," he whispered, low-voiced.

"I think he resigned. There's a new surgeon general now, one that doesn't look like a Dutch admiral."

"If you say so. I had thought that the postmaster general or the Attorney General would be next, but they have continued to cling to power. Perhaps they are in league with the President of Vice."

"Right," Remo said, looking out at the mountainous ground below. "That Postmaster General. He's a pretender to the throne if one ever lived."

Chiun arranged his silken skirts, saying, "I am pleased you agree with me. We will bring this matter to Smith's attention at a propitious moment. More emperors have been toppled from their thrones by military coups than popular revolts. It is an unfortunate truism of history."

The engine whine changed pitch and Remo felt

the pressure build up in his ears. He opened his mouth slightly and his eardrums cleared instantly.

A mountaintop poked up on Remo's side of the plane. Another appeared on the opposite side. The plane began buffeting.

"Looks like we're here," Remo said as the plane tipped its right wing, showing the sprawling Valley of Mexico below.

"What ruins are those?" Chiun demanded, pointing to a vast jumble of gray stone dominated by a great flat-sided pyramid.

"One of the Aztec ruins, I guess," Remo guessed.

"We never worked for them," Chiun said, dismissing the entire sweep of Aztec civilization with a papery frown.

"Too bad," Remo said. "They were right up your alley. Made the czars look like muppets."

On the ground, Remo went to change his American dollars for pesos so he could use the airport pay phone.

He returned to the Master of Sinanju with his pockets bulging with heavy coins.

"This place is worse than Great Britain," Remo complained as he fed coins into the pay-phone slot. "They got a million different coins and no paper money under a five-peso bill. If they ever get around to abolishing the dollar bill back home, I vote we move to Canada."

"There is no work in Canada," Chiun pointed out. "Nothing goes on up there."

Remo grinned. "Sounds like retirement paradise."

Smith came on the line, his voice lemony and sharp.

"They cannot find the President's body," he said glumly.

"Does that mean he could have survived?" Remo asked, hope rising in his voice.

"Impossible," Smith said. "Air crashes of that severity rarely allow for survivors. We have to operate under the assumption that we have lost our chief executive."

"Damn," Remo said. "Is there anything Chiun and I can do?"

"Yes, I've booked you on a Mexicana flight to the town of Tampico. That's the staging area we're using to process the crash site. You're now Remo Jones, a cultural attaché with the U.S. embassy in Mexico City."

"That means I'm CIA, right?"

"You will contact Comandante Oscar Odio of the Mexican Federal Security Directorate, the DFS, in Tampico. The Mexicans are requesting an on-site observer. Soon they will be demanding it. Your task will be to handle their on-site person. That will be your entrée to the crash site."

"Sounds like we've just pulled baby-sitting duty," Remo grumbled.

"Call it what you will," Smith returned. "I want you in the area in case something breaks."

"What about the Colombians?"

"We'll close the barn door later. Just follow orders."

"You're a prince, Smith." Remo hung up. He turned. Chiun was looking up at him, his head cocked, his hazel eyes narrow.

"What?" Remo asked, placing his hands on his hips.

"Why did you refer to Smith as a prince?" he asked suspiciously.

"Now, don't get the wrong idea. It's just—"

Chiun's hand shot up. "No lies. Speak the truth

only, Remo. If Smith is making his move now, I must know it. Matters of succession require delicacy and correctness. I will not be party to a sloppy palace coup."

"It's just an expression," Remo shouted. And noticing that he was attracting attention in the busy terminal, he continued in a low, controlled voice, "I was pulling Smith's leg."

"Over the telephone?" Chiun said skeptically.

Remo looked ceilingward. "It's another expression."

"I do not want to hear expressions or excuses," Chiun snapped loudly. "I demand the truth."

"Okay, okay," Remo relented. "Congratulations. You've figured it out. It *is* a coup. Smith is deposing the Postmaster General. All those free stamps just for the taking have pushed Smith to the brink."

"How does eliminating the President figure into this?" Chiun went on in a mollified tone as they sought the Mexicana Airlines counter.

"It's really, really complicated," Remo said distractedly.

"Ah," said Chiun, and lapsed into silence. Then: "You may explain it to me on our flight. I assume we are going to fly again?"

"Yeah, we're going to the crash site."

"Yes, of course. To cover up the evidence of Smith's plotting. A wise move, and politically expedient."

Harold W. Smith made the appropriate phone calls to the State Department, which contacted the U.S. embassy in Mexico City, which in turn put in a call to Comandante Oscar Odio's office in Tampico.

So when Remo Williams presented himself at the headquarters of the Dirección Federal de Seguridad in Tampico, no one asked to see his identification as he entered the white Spanish-colonial building.

A blue-uniformed guard at the main desk, however, looked at Chiun quizzically as he listened to Remo identify himself and then escorted them to the *comandante*'s office.

Tampico Zone Comandante Oscar Odio didn't ask Remo for his identification either. He smiled broadly under a mustache so thick it looked as if it had been grown in a refrigerator. The first words out of his mouth were a silken, *"Bienvenidos, señores."*

"Hi," Remo said sourly.

Comandante Odio looked at Remo's casual attire, and his attitude cooled.

"You are the attaché from the American embassy," he said, his black jewellike eyes gleaming. "Dressed like that?"

"I was on vacation," Remo told him with a straight face. "In Cancún. Didn't have time to change."

"And this man?" Comandante Odio indicated the Master of Sinanju.

"This is Chiun," Remo said without skipping a beat. "My interpreter."

Odio frowned. "He is not Spanish."

"Neither are you, Mexican," the Master of Sinanju snapped in perfect Spanish.

Comandante Oscar Odio winced. "I see. Still, you will have no need for this man, I assure you. For I speak impeccable English, as you can plainly hear, Señor Yones."

"Jones."

"Yes. That is what I have said. Yones."

"He comes anyway," Remo said flatly. "Or none of us goes."

Comandante Odio stiffened. "As you say," he said, the smoothness leaving his voice again. "A helicopter awaits us. As soon as the representative from the

Federal Judicial Police arrives, we will be on our way."

"The who?" Remo said suddenly.

"I represent the Federal Security Directorate. The Federales have insisted on having an observer also."

"Look," Remo said testily, "this is an emergency. Do we have to stand on ceremony?"

"This is our country, Señor Yones. Not yours. Please be good enough to enjoy our hospitality while we wait. Would you care for a drink?" Odio reached into a desk drawer and extracted a large bottle. "Tequila?"

"No," Remo said flatly.

Odio turned to the Master of Sinanju, saying, "You, señor?"

"It has a worm in it," Chiun sniffed.

A peculiar smile settled over Odio's handsome features as he returned the bottle to its place unopened.

Remo looked out the window, where an olive helicopter with side-mounted machine guns sat under a tall ahuehuete tree. Worry rode his hard features. The President dead. Terrorists involved. He wondered where the Vice-President was now and if they were still keeping the news from him.

6

Deep within the Sierra Madres, Walid cocked an ear to the roof over his head and listened to the clatter. It was thin, and growing thinner.

"The *helikobters* are not so loud now," he ventured.

"The roof," Jalid observed, "it is covered with sand. Perfect camouflage against the Americans."

Abu Al-Kalbin shoved another wooden spoonful of steamed rice into his mouth. He wolfed it down greedily.

"Are you sure this will help?" he demanded of Walid and Jalid, white grains clinging from his half-open mouth.

"The rice, it absorbs water in the bowels," Walid said sincerely.

"Soon you will have firm solid stools," Jalid added, smiling.

"At this moment, I want that more than anything," Abu Al-Kalbin said fervently. "Even more than the Qaddafi Peace Prize."

He upended the bowl to let the clumpy rice tumble into his yawning mouth like dead white ants.

They spoke in Arabic, so that the President of the hated United States could not understand them. The

President sat in a rude wood chair in the tar-paper-and-tin safe house nestled in the Sierra Madres, which had been arranged for them by their Colombian employer. From the smell, they guessed it was a marijuana stash house.

The President sat, his head tipped forward and resting on his chin. A colorful embroidered blindfold shielded his eyes; his hands were bound to the two crosspieces of the chair back with twine. His feet were looped to the front chair legs with his own belt. It was a very fine belt. Abu Al-Kalbin hoped to keep it as a souvenir once they had sold the man into servitude.

Over in one dim corner, Walid was playing with a video camera. He pointed it at the President, and Jalid quickly jumped into the frame, throwing his arms around the President's thin shoulders, striking a pose and showing strong white teeth.

Pausing in his greedy rice devouring, Abu Al-Kalbin noticed Jalid's naked teeth and hissed a warning.

"You fool! Put on your kaffiyeh! If these films fall into bad hands, your foolish face will be on every wall and police bulletin board from here to Cairo."

Stung, Jalid reached behind him and pulled the tail of his fringed kaffiyeh around to his mouth. He restruck his cocky pose.

"How will we get him out of the country?" Jalid asked as Walid filmed him.

"I have not figured out that part," Abu Al-Kalbin mumbled through a mouthful of rice. "I am too busy setting my disgestive tract to rights. Curse these Mexican dishes. They go down like fire and come out of you the same way."

Walid and Jalid burst into laughter. Their raucous

merriment died when a low groan escaped the President's compressed lips.

All heads turned to the President.

At that exact moment, there came a knock at the door.

All heads swiveled to the door.

"Who?" Abu Al-Kalbin blurted, rice grains dropping onto his lap.

"The Colombian?" Jalid suggested. "El Padrino?"

"He would not come here," Abu Al-Kalbin hissed. "Not while the U.S. *helikobters* comb the skies." He indicated the door with a sharp inclination of his head.

Walid grabbed up his AK-47 and went to answer the door. Jalid followed him with the whirring videocam, while a second groan escaped the lips of the President of the United States.

Walid snapped off the safety of his automatic rifle. He held it low on his hip with his right hand, set himself in a wide-legged combat stance, and reached out to throw open the door with his left.

At a nod from Abu Al-Kalbin, he yanked open the door.

He never fired.

For framed within the door was a tall blue-eyed, vacuously smiling man of young middle age.

Walid's jaw dropped. He recognized the face of the man in the doorway. His astonishment caused him to hold his fire.

And while his stupefied brain was registering the seemingly impossible sight of Robert Redford at the door, the American actor calmly reached over his shoulder and extracted a nine iron from his golf bag. He lifted it to his shoulder like a baseball player.

The club came around with such easy grace that

Walid never saw the aluminum pole that dashed his
brains out of his skull, sending hot yellowish brain
matter splattering like grease.

A splash of it struck Abu Al-Kalbin in the face,
momentarily blinding him. Curds of it dropped into
his rice bowl, which fell from his hands and cracked
on the floor.

Abu Al-Kalbin shot to his feet, pawing at the organic matter in his furiously batting eyes as the at-
tacker stepped into the tar-paper shack, hurling his
mangled nine iron away and selecting a driver.

The driver caught Abu Al-Kalbin in the jaw, knocking it off with a bone-meal crunch. The driver went
back to the wielder's shoulder. This time it drove in
for the exposed neck. It connected with such inhuman force that it tore Abu Al-Kalbin's head off his
shoulders.

The head struck and bounced off the wall.

Jalid watched all of this through the range finder of
his video camera. The range finder made the rapid
series of violent actions seem as if they were very,
very far away. Jalid retreated to a far wall, still recording the sight as if the camera offered him not
only distance and perspective but also protection.
Many war correspondents caught in free-fire zones
had made that mistake. A few survived it.

Jalid did not survive his.

A putter lifted in very bad form like an ax about to
chop down. It struck Jalid on the exact top of the
head, separating skull plates that had been fused
since Jalid was only six months old.

The golf-club wielder released the putter. It went
down with the corpse, sticking up from the broken
bleeding head like a fifth appendage. It quivered. So
did Jalid's other appendages. The ones whose nerves

were receiving electrically disrupted signals from its
disrupted brain.

Ignoring the corpse, the man walked over to the
bound form of the President of the United States,
whose head groggily lifted off his chest. He craned
his long Ichabod Crane neck as if trying to see past
his blindfold.

"Hello?" he croaked, his voice anxious. "I can't
see. Where am I? Can anyone hear me? I hear you
moving around. Hello? Answer me!"

The President of the United States felt strong fingers touch his forehead, plucking away the blindfold
with an easy rip that broke the fabric as clean as a
knife. He lifted his face. The early-morning sunlight
coming through the single window was not strong,
but it hurt his eyes nevertheless. He looked up at
the figure that towered over him, his vision gradually
clearing.

The figure spoke. It said, "Hello is all right."

"Dan?" the President of the United States croaked
in disbelief.

7

The woman in the fawn-colored uniform had the saddest face Remo Williams had ever seen on a woman.

She ignored Chiun and himself as she stepped into the office of Zone Comandante Oscar Odio, executed a crisp salute, and announced herself.

"Federal Yudicial Police Officer Guadalupe Mazatl reporting, Comandate."

Comandante Odio returned the salute with only a slightly annoyed expression on his face.

"We have been awaiting you, *señorita*," he murmured.

"Officer," Guadalupe Mazatl corrected. She was a short woman, perhaps only five-foot-four, with a sturdy body that made up in rounded strength what it lacked in grace. She had coffee-colored skin, strong high cheekbones, and extremely black eyes. They might have come from the same military store as her shiny black boots and gunbelt. Her dark hair was short and severe.

"And these are the *gringos*?" she said, indicating Remo and Chiun with a toss of her black hair.

"You must excuse Officer Mazatl," Comandante

Odio said, throwing the woman a hard glance while bestowing a smooth smile upon Remo and Chiun. "She has evidently left her manners behind."

"My manners are fine," Mazatl snapped. "It is the *gringos* who have swooped down upon us, despoiling our sovereignity. Just as they did in Panama."

"Look," Remo said tensely. "Can we just go?"

"Naturally," Comandante Odio returned with a quick bowing of his head. He took his service cap off his desk and put it on. A white silk scarf went around the neck of his blue uniform. "Follow me, *por favor*," he said, adding mirrored aviator sunglasses to the ensemble.

Officer Mazatl fell in behind them without a word.

As they walked to the waiting helicopter, Comandante Odio whispered to Remo, "My apologies, *señor*. The Federales are notoriously lacking in pleasantness. The few women especially so. And corrupt."

"I'll keep that in mind," Remo promised, inwardly wanting only to get on with it.

The helicopter lifted off with a clattery whir and angled toward the foreboding Sierra Madres. Comandante Odio himself piloted the ship. Remo sat up front beside him, looking down as the brown ridges floated under the ship's skids. His Sinanju-trained eyes raked the barren peaks, looking for signs of life—or death. He saw neither. There were roads and railroad tracks crossing the range, but the peaks and mountainsides looked as if the First Wind had scoured them clean and no foot had known them since.

In the back, Guadalupe Mazatl put a question to the Master of Sinanju.

"Are you Yapanese?"

"No. What are you?"

"I am an *azteca*," she said with a trace of pride. "*Ciento por ciento*. One hundred percent Aztec."

"You are proud of this?" Chiun asked doubtfully.

"I am."

"Then why do you look so sad?"

"I am not sad. I am Mexican," said Guadalupe Mazatl, as if that explained everything. "What are you?"

The Master of Sinanju pretended not to hear her over the rotor clatter. It was exactly what the rude woman who dressed like a man deserved after calling him a Japanese. No wonder his ancestors had not seen fit to exploit the Aztec market.

Presently the crash site came into view. Comandante Odio talked to the orbiting Air Force helicopters, was cleared to land, and set the chopper down well away from the knots of investigative teams.

Remo stepped out onto the crusty sand. The caterwaul of argumentative shouting lifted over the dying rotor whine.

An Air Force officer in a blue uniform was shouting down a man in mufti. The man in mufti was getting red in the face. He looked like he was about to explode. When the Air Force officer paused in his tirade to catch a breath, he did.

"You listen to me, Corporal!" he began.

"Colonel."

"To me, it's all the same," the other shot back. "The President of the United States is technically missing. Not dead. Missing. That makes it a Secret Service matter."

"Last I heard, the Secret Service didn't have helicopter search capabilities. You want to hitch a ride in our birds, mister, that's fine. Otherwise, you remain on the ground. Read me?"

"We'll see about this!" And the Secret Service man marched off in a huff to another civilian, who handed him a cellular telephone.

Remo walked up to the colonel.

"You in charge?" he demanded.

"Who the hell are you?"

"Remo Jones. U.S. embassy."

The colonel subsided. His voice was still testy as he asked, "And who are these people?" He pointed to the Master of Sinanju and the Mexican representatives.

"Chiun's my interpreter. The others can introduce themselves. I want a look inside the plane."

The colonel shook his head. "Sorry. The damn NTSB has it roped off. Won't let anyone inside. The FBI is having fits. They say it's a terrorist bombing. And there's the NTSB. They say it's an air disaster, and therefore falls under their purview."

Over by the broken tail, two civilians stood shouting at one another. One wore a blue jacket and baseball cap labeled: NTSB.

"I take it that's the flip side of this mess?" Remo said.

"It's a bureaucratic nightmare!" the colonel snapped. "No one's ever had a situation like this. It's an air disaster, a possible kidnapping, and an international incident all rolled into one, with terroristic overtones. No ones knows where the jurisdictional lines should be drawn."

"It's also a national catastrophe," Remo said. "Come on, Chiun."

Officer Mazatl started to follow, but was stopped by the colonel. That led to a sudden argument over Mexican territoriality, with Comandante Odio trying in vain to placate both sides.

The Master of Sinanju drew up beside Remo, and Remo marched toward the argument, his fists tight.

"That woman spoke words of wisdom to me," Chiun said.

"What are those?"

"She says that the Mexican DFS is notoriously corrupt and not to trust the *comandante*."

"Funny. That's what the *comandante* said about her," Remo muttered. "Nobody seems to care about what happened out here. Just how it affects their freaking turf."

"Do not take it so hard, my son. You have seen many Presidents come and go in your young life. How is this different?"

"One," Remo said tightly, "we don't know that he's dead yet. Two, it happened on our watch."

"While we were doing our duty elsewhere," Chiun pointed out. "This is all Smith's fault. Had he possessed good information, this embarrassment could have been avoided."

"You too?" Remo snapped. "The President is missing, and all everybody is concerned about is their backsides. Wonderful."

"Remo!" Chiun said, blowing out his cheeks in anger. But when his pupil did not stop to engage in an argument, the Master of Sinanju hurried to join him. He said nothing. He had never seen his pupil this way. Perhaps Remo had voted for the man. They approached the two shouting whites.

"Look, Lunkhead, or Lunkin," Bill Holland was screaming, "I'll say it once more. The FBI can observe. It cannot—repeat, cannot—participate in processing the site!"

Remo waded into the argument between Bill Holland of the National Transportation Safety Board and

Agent Lunkin of the FBI like a referee breaking up two hockey players. He took them by the backs of their necks and shook them until their teeth rattled.

"Shut up! Both of you! Now!"

"Who are you?" Bill Holland demanded, unable to break Remo's steel-strong finger grip on his neck.

The FBI agent said nothing. He had inadvertently bitten his own tongue in the shaking and was busy stemming the flow of blood by holding it with his fingers.

"Remo Jones. Cultural attaché, U.S. embassy. I'm here as an observer, and what I see stinks. I want a report."

"I don't report to you," Holland said sullenly.

Remo's fingers dug into Holland's spine and suddenly he was reporting freely.

"She was shot down," he gasped. "We found a Stinger fire unit in the hills. We've accounted for all passengers and crew, except one. There's a body missing."

"The President's?" Remo demanded.

"Could be. Some of the corpses are so mutilated it's impossible to tell until the forensic team goes to work."

"So the President might have survived?" Remo asked in a quieter tone, after releasing Holland's neck.

Holland shook his head. "If he was aboard when it came down, he's gone. You can go to your grave believing it."

"I'd rather see for myself. I'm going in."

"The forensic team has not been inside yet," he warned.

"Ask me if I care," Remo said, starting off.

Before Bill Holland could reply, a civilian helicop-

ter clattered into view over a mountaintop. It settled
to the ground, making their clothes ripple.

"That will be them," Holland said, shielding his
eyes against the high Mexican sun. "We can walk
through the site with them—if you've got the stomach for it."

"I've seen worse than this," Remo said, watching
as two gangling men in identical black business suits
emerged from the back of a Bell Jet Ranger. They
each carried a black briefcase. At the sight of Holland's lifted arm, they made a beeline for him.

"That's Murray and Murphy, the Merry Morti-
cians," Holland told Remo out of the side of his
mouth. "You'll see in a minute why we call them
that."

Remo stood about, arms folded impatiently as Holland greeted the pair. Together they entered the
broken blue-and-white shell that had been *Air Force
One*.

"Never mind this one," Holland told Murray and
Murphy as they stepped over a body. "He's already
identified. Did you bring the President's dental
records?"

"You bet," Murray said.

"He should be easy to ID," Murphy added. "All
we need to see are the teeth. He had a gold-filled
back molar. Right side."

"No, the left," Murray corrected.

"A gold-filled molar, anyway," Murphy said in a
genial voice.

Inside the downed aircraft, they picked their way
to the presidential section. The craft's interior had
been stripped down to the braces and wiring by the
impact. They stopped before a mangled corpse. The
metallic smell of blood filled the narrow confines.

"Where's his head?" Murray wanted to know.

"Hasn't been found," Holland said.

"Without the head," Murphy added in a disappointed voice, "we don't have our gold-filled molar. Somebody better find the head."

"That's not the President," Remo inserted. "Must be a journalist. Look at the cheap suit."

Everyone looked. They all agreed with Remo's supposition. They moved on to the next body.

The next one had been practically rendered into raw meat.

"What happened to him?" Remo asked, taken aback by the mutilation.

"There are a lot of anomalies on this one," Holland told him. "Never seen anything like it."

"Oh, well, time to get to work," Murray said, setting his briefcase beside the barely human remains.

Murphy did the same. They opened their briefcases in concert-hall synchronization and with careful fingers drew on identical rubber surgical gloves. Then they proceeded to poke and prod the exposed viscera of the abdomen like children playing in mud.

Bill Holland turned away.

Remo signaled Chiun to keep Holland distracted, and moved through the cabin. He stepped over bodies, quickly dismissing those that were too short or too fat or the wrong sex. He noticed the damage to the radarscope and other equipment, and although he possessed no air-crash investigative experience, he intuitively understood patterns of destruction and realized that he was looking at manmade, not natural destruction, in many places. Kneeling, he examined obvious bullet wounds.

Remo went back to join Chiun and Bill Holland in the open air. On the way out, he smelled the sour sick smell that he had noticed only subliminally on the way in.

He stopped, tracking it with his nose. A messy, trampled-on stain in the dark blue rug, directly over the Presidential Seal. It looked like puppy excrement.

Remo rejoined the others.

"I don't think the President's body is in there," Remo told Holland.

"I had a crash once," Holland mused, "where a DC-4 went down in the Rockies. Up in Montana. We combed the crash radius and for six miles in all directions, collected every rivet and wire of the airframe, and every lost soul about, except one. The copilot. It was the wildest thing we'd ever seen. Totally unexplainable." Holland's eyes went out of focus, as if he were reliving the experience.

"Yeah?" Remo prompted.

"Until we went through the passenger manifests," Holland added firmly. "Found out the copilot's girlfriend was flying in coach. Started me thinking. What if he had gone back to talk to her? What if the plane turned over in flight?"

"He went out a window?" Remo suggested.

"No, out the astrodome. The aircraft encountered turbulance and inverted while he was walking up the aisle, and down he went. We found his body thirty miles from the crash site. What the coyotes left."

"*Air Force One* have an astrodome?" Remo wanted to know.

"No," Bill Holland said, looking out toward the mountains. "It's totally inexplicable." He turned to Remo. "But there'll be a reasonable explanation for this one too. And we'll find it. If the FBI, Secret Service, and Air Force just stay off our back long enough for us to do our jobs," he added.

Saying that, Bill Holland sucked in a deep breath and reentered the wreckage.

Remo glanced over to the Master of Sinanju. Chiun's head was up. He sniffed the dry desert air, his hands tucked away in his joined kimono sleeves. He looked like a scarlet silk genie.

Remo fixed his eye on *Air Force One's* tail assembly, which lay nearby, tilted onto one bent stabilizer. The ground was hard brown sand. The kind that formed a cracked crust after rainstorms, the kind that would not show footprints, but breaks in the crust.

His eyes tracked a necklace of such breaks going off to the horizon.

"Looks like someone headed off in that direction," Remo ventured. "South."

"Yes. The direction of the awful smell."

"Smell?"

"Did you not smell it, Remo? That belly-sickness stink?"

"Yeah. I smelled it back in the plane. Almost stepped in it, too."

"It is fainter out here. But to those with senses such as ours, it is an odor that could be followed to the one who reeks of it."

"Good thinking," Remo said, looking around slowly. "We could cover a lot more ground by helicopter."

"True. But we could not follow the scent from the air," Chiun pointed out.

"Yeah. And we'd be bogged down in a lot of bureaucratic infighting too."

Remo considered the situation. He rotated his thick wrists impatiently, a habit he had when he was thinking. He was thinking furiously.

Over by the Mexican helicopter, the Air Force colonel, Officer Guadalupe Mazatl, and Comandante

Odio were talking earnestly. Odio's smile was turned up to one hundred candlepower. It seemed to be working. Officer Mazatl and the colonel were scowling at one another, but no longer shouting.

Finally Remo made a decision.

"Let's cut out," he told Chiun. "Subtly."

They began to drift off, trying not to seem to be obvious as they moved away from the crash site. The NTSB personnel milling around the site were so preoccupied with their work—or their arguments— that no one noticed that they had slipped away.

Until Officer Guadalupe Mazatl looked up from her huddle with Comandant Odio and the *yanqui* colonel and noticed the figure of the white *gringo* and the yellow old man receding in the distance.

She took a step back from the huddle. The men were ignoring her. Officer Mazatl worked her way to the other side of the crash site, ignoring, and being ignored in turn, by the *gringos*.

They ignored her until she was far from the site, and after she had melted into the sierra, they did not miss her.

8

The President of the United States was amazed at the change in his Vice-President.

The man had been, frankly, an embarrassment from the day the presidential nominee had announced his selection before an eager Atlanta campaign crowd, and the then-Vice-President-designate had hugged him like a long-lost brother, shouting inanities like "Go get 'em!" That started all the Son of the President jokes.

Then came the National Guard enlistment story, but the President—then merely his party's nominee—had hung tough. And it had paid off. The National Guard thing had blown over.

The jokes, however, had never blown over. Every stand-up comedian had a phone book full of them. How the Vice-President had kept his home state safe from the Vietcong during the war. How he resembled Robert Redford. How he was for sure no Jack Kennedy. The golfing jokes. And the cruel one that had it that the Secret Service were under orders to shoot the Vice-President if anything happened to the President.

It got so bad that even the Secret Service had

gone along with it. They had code-named him "Scorecard."

And yet, after the early trying months on the campaign trail, it had worked out. For the President. After the election, the media continued to lampoon the Vice-President. And the more of a lightning rod he became, the less fun the media made of the President of the United States. His approval rating went through the roof.

It had been a good choice after all. And in the privacy of the Oval Office, the President himself had fallen into the habit of repeating the better zingers he had over heard. Strictly in fun.

He was not laughing now.

He had discovered new respect when the Vice-President removed his blindfold and said, in a strained, halting voice, "Hello is all right."

Well, it was no big deal. The Vice-President always had problems with his syntax. The President himself had had to be coached by his handlers not to mangle his own sentence structure and to keep his often-jerky body language under control.

But when the Vice-President, his eyes acrinkle over that fixed smile of his, bent down and pulled his leg bonds apart with his bare hands, the President had been really impressed.

"Gee, I never knew you were so strong," the President had blurted out foolishly. It was the only thing he could think to say.

The Vice-President stepped behind him and performed the same Samson-like feat on his bound hands. The wooden chair back actually came apart under the grip of his firm hands like a balsa sculpture.

The President had to be helped to his feet.

"This is amazing!" he had said. "Been working out, have you?"

"Survival, this is," the Vice-President had said.

"Yes, adrenaline. I understand. It does incredible things, really incredible. But, Dan, how did you get down here? How did you find me?"

"Protect you. My mission is to."

The poor guy sounded like Yoda from *Star Wars*, but the President understood his meaning.

"Take a deep breath," he had said as feeling returned to his numb limbs. "Calm down. Tell me what the heck's going on. The last thing I remember is *Air Force One* going down. Then I sorta blacked out."

"We survived."

"You mean I survived. You weren't aboard."

"Surviving is the most important element in survival. To survive is to survive. To have survived is to be in existence."

"Yeah, I think I get your drift," the President had said, patting his Vice-President on one nerve-rigid shoulder. The poor fella was really rattled. He looked around the dim cabin for something cool to drink, possibly to throw over the Vice-President. He looked really overheated, despite his fixed, too-perfect smile. Not only that, but his suit didn't match. He was wearing a brown coat over navy-blue slacks. He also sported the worst haircut this side of Borneo. Perhaps it was the Vice-President's attempt at being incognito, he mused.

Then the President of the United States noticed the bodies.

"Oh, my God."

The kaffiyehs were all the President needed to see to know that they were Middle Eastern terrorists of some sort. In a way, it was a relief. Middle Eastern terrorists had never directly threatened a United

States President. Colombian narco-terrorists, on the other hand, were capable of anything. Most of them used their own product.

"What happened to these guys?" the President croaked.

"They threatened our survival. Their survival became a threat to your survival. Their survival was interrupted."

The Vice-President lifted a driver from the golf bag that, for the first time, the President noticed slung over his shoulder.

"You took them out with a driver?" he asked, incredulous.

"Was it the correct tool?"

"To tee off, yeah, but for this . . ." The President looked around the shack. It had been a long time since he had seen dead bodies. Not since World War II.

"I am very creative," the Vice-President said simply.

"Where exactly am I?" the President asked suddenly.

"With me. With you I always am. With you I will always be." The Vice-President replaced the driver like Conan the Barbarian holstering an over-the-back broadsword.

The President put both hands on the Vice-President's shoulders, once again amazed by the unyielding hardness of his musculature.

"That's a really, really noble sentiment, and I appreciate it. I really do."

"The task of serving the President is a task," the Vice-President said with all the warmth of a Swiss watch ticking.

"Right," the President remarked. "That's fine. You take another deep breath. I want to look around a bit."

A sudden hand stopped the President. It was the Vice-President.

"There is no time," he said in a mechanical mono-
tone. "Must escape. Must survive. If you survive, I
will continue to survive. Separated, must not be.
We."

The President took in that unalterable fixed smile
and decided to say yes. It could be the Vice-President
was verging on hysteria. His eyes were definitely
glassy, and instead of making sense, he was babbling
more and more.

"Whatever you say. I trust you."

"Trust," the Vice-President repeated. "We cannot
trust anyone until we are reunited."

"I miss my family too. Whatever you say."

"I say we go. Must return to the United States,
your home."

"Okay," the President said slowly. "Let's go."

Only then did the too-firm hand release the President's windbreaker sleeve.

The President stepped into the sunlight first, the
Vice-President walking closely behind, like a child
pretending to be his shadow. He was met by a
bleak brown expanse of desert and distant mountains.

"Looks like we got a long walk," the President said
unhappily.

They had not gone more than a quarter-mile when
the clatter of a distant helicopter came from the
nearby mountains.

The President lifted waving arms. "Hey!" he called.

Without warning, the Vice-President pushed him
down behind a great spike-leaved ground plant that
resembled a giant artichoke. His hands squeezed off
his cries for help. He kept him pressed to the ground
until the clatter dissipated.

Only then did the Vice-President's heavy hand
leave the small of his back.

Getting to his feet, the President dusted off his windbreaker, saying, "I appreciate what you're doing for me, but not so rough next time. Okay?"

"There will be more machines. Hurry we must."

"Gee, I don't know. Maybe they're friendly."

"They threaten our mutual survival."

The President's face twisted in concern. "More terrorists?"

"We must reach optimum position of safety. Come."

They trudged on. The sun climbed in the sky. The cool morning air warmed. The President grew parched and hungry.

The Vice-President found solutions to both of those problems. He uprooted a rubbery plant with his bare hands and squeezed precious drops of water into the President's eager mouth as if from a sponge.

Then he stalked a rattlesnake with a putter, decapitating it with one swift, sure blow. He broke off the head, and then skinned the snake by pulling on the skin with one hand and on the exposed neck meat with the other. The snake came apart like an entwined rope.

The President declined the raw meat with a polite, "No. You go ahead."

"I am self-sustaining, thank you."

They went on.

"Gotta hand it to you, Dan," the President said as they skirted the base of a mountain range. "You amaze me. These survival skills of yours—pick them up in the National Guard, did you?"

"I have known how to survive since I was created," the Vice-President replied, placing one ear to the flat parched ground.

The statement surprised the President for two reasons. Not the least of which was that it was the first coherent sentence the Vice-President had spoken all morning.

The Vice-President listened in silence. He shot to his feet suddenly and, with a combination of speed and stealth that astonished the President, gathered him up in a fireman's carry.

He began running.

His head dangling upside down, the President was unable to see where he was being taken. The sandy ground raced by so fast that he got dizzy. If he hadn't known it was an impossibility, the President would have sworn they were running at a clip of over sixty miles an hour. He closed his eyes. He was grateful he hadn't eaten that snake. It wouldn't have stayed down in this kind of activity.

Several bouncing minutes later, the sound of a train startled the President into opening his eyes.

The ground was moving, if anything, still faster.

And the sound of the train grew louder and louder and louder until it was on top of the President. He craned his fear-twisted face around.

He saw an old diesel engine, making good time. The President barely registered its massive bulk, and then the sky was in his face. He felt weightless, disconnected. Then every bone in his lanky body shook with unexpected impact and he gave out an involuntary yell.

For a nightmarish instant he thought they had been sucked under the big steel wheels.

Instead, he found himself gently deposited on a hot rattling metal surface.

"Where the hell are we?" the President demanded, pulling himself together.

The answer was all around him.

The President found himself sprawled on the platform of a caboose. The smell of diesel smoke was in his nostrils. His teeth shook and the train went clickety-clack on the rail segments. Grit popped under the spinning steel wheels. A mournful whistle gave out.

On either side of them, huge mountains reared up. They were traveling through a mountain range.

"Is it safe here?" the President asked, hanging on to the railed back of the platform.

"Safe here it is," the Vice-President said, his fixed-smile face lifting to the sky, visible above the caboose's roof overhang.

Two helicopters zipped past like harridan vultures. They flew low, but from this vantage point the President could make out only their sun-shadowed underbellies. There were no markings visible.

"This is awful," the President groaned. "We're in deep doo-doo."

"I do not understand 'doo-doo,' " the Vice-President said without evident humor.

"You will," the President said unhappily as the desolate landscape unfolded around them. "Down here, it's everywhere you go."

9

They could smell the bodies before they sighted the desolate shack.

Remo and Chiun had stepped up on a tumble of dusty rocks in an effort to see more clearly.

Chiun spotted the forlorn-looking shack in the brown foothills.

"The smell of death," he intoned, pointing. "It comes from there."

"Come on!" Remo said, rushing for the cabin.

"I do not understand your unseemly haste, Remo," Chiun said as they sprinted through the scrub desert, their light feet leaving only the merest prints on the sand.

"He's the President," Remo hissed.

"But we work for Smith."

"And Smith works for the President," Remo added.

"But is not answerable to him."

"That's the way the organization was set up in the first place. So no one could abuse CURE. America isn't a police state."

"A good thought. Only Smith is privileged to abuse the organization."

"Smith would never do that. That's why he was chosen for the job."

"He is a mere man, and therefore corruptible."

"I'll give Smith this," Remo said. "He does his job. Sometimes too well. But he does it."

"I still fail to understand your concern. You have lost a President. But they are like rugs. You dispose of them every four years. Sometimes every eight years. But they are clearly superfluous. I have heard some boast that any waif can grow up to be President. If that is true, then there is nothing special about any of them. They are not a bloodline, so no dynasty is threatened by the death of this President. He is voted in. And is voted out. So? This one has been voted out by terrorists."

"Terrorists don't vote," Remo said grimly. "And I don't believe he's dead. Yet."

"I smell death," Chiun warned. "You should be prepared."

Remo should have slowed down when he got within range of the cabin. But the Master of Sinanju saw with a frown that he did not. Remo plunged into the open door like some ninja blunderer.

Chiun had no choice but to follow him in, and he did.

He found Remo ranging around the single room, upsetting tables and chairs and ignoring the three Middle Eastern corpses that were flung around the interior like so many unwanted dolls.

"No sign of him!" Remo said anxiously.

The Master of Sinanju strode immediately to one of the chairs Remo had upended in his controlled fury.

It was damaged, and lengths of snapped twine clung to the pieces.

"He has been here," Chiun said loudly. "And he was alive. No one binds a corpse to a chair."

Remo stopped what he was doing. He accepted frayed ends of twine from Chiun's long-nailed fingers.

"So who freed him?" Remo wondered. "And where did they go?"

"I do not know," said the Master of Sinanju, looking about the room. His eyes gleamed and he brushed past his pupil. Remo followed him with his eyes.

The Master of Sinanju reached down and lifted a black video camrecorder.

"Probably taken from *Air Force One*," Remo suggested.

"How do you work this device?"

"If it's one of those that give you instant playback, you rewind it and just press the trigger like on a gun. Then you look through the viewfinder."

"I cannot find this so-called viewfinder," Chiun complained.

"Give it here."

The Master of Sinanju retreated away from Remo's outreaching hand, saying, "No! I will do this myself."

Remo folded his arms in annoyance. "You won't see anything useful anyway. These ragheads probably stole it just to hock it. They wouldn't actually record the abduction. They're not idiots."

The Master of Sinanju paid no attention to his pupil's prattle. He found the proper buttons and lifted the device to one eager hazel eye. He depressed the trigger.

And before his eyes an amazing procession of images was displayed.

"I see the President!" Chiun cried in triumph.

Remo started. "You do?"

"He is answering questions put to him by unseen interrogaters."

"Oh," Remo said, subsiding, "press-conference stuff."

"Wait! There is more!"

"What?" Remo said, reaching out again. Chiun faded back even though one eye was closed and the other was glued to the viewfinder.

"I see these three corpses lying dead about us, but in life."

"You do?"

"Yes. And they are recording the abduction of the true President, who appears to be unconscious, much like your President of Vice, except that the President's eyes are closed."

"He's alive!" Remo blurted.

"They are carrying him off, the imbeciles."

"Yeah?"

"Now they are posing with him," Chiun squeaked. "The President is bound to the chair with twine and a belt."

"Are they torturing him?"

"If he were awake, it could be called that," Chiun snapped.

Remo's fists clenched. "No!"

"They are capering around him like baboons, making inane comments and acting in jest. They are truly imbeciles." Chiun stopped speaking.

"What's happening now?" Remo demanded.

"I am coming to that," Chiun said, turning the video camera this way and that, as if to get a better view. "Ah!" Chiun breathed. Then, in a hard voice: "Oh! Oh, no!"

"What? What?" Remo asked anxiously.

"It is a plot!" Chiun cried in triumph. "I was right."

"What? About what?"

"Behold," the Master of Sinanju said, quickly passing the video recorder to Remo.

Remo caught it up to his eyes. He pressed the trigger. He saw the late Abu Al-Kalbin at the exact moment he was beheaded by a number-one wood, wielded by familiar hands.

"It's the Vice-President," Remo said in disbelief.

"The schemer!" Chiun added indignantly.

"My God, he's pulverizing these terrorists."

"A subterfuge," Chiun cried. "He is disposing of his underlings so they cannot betray him. We will be vindicated in Emperor Smith's eyes, after all. He sent us on a ferocious goose quest."

"Wild-goose chase."

"The very same!" Chiun's voice rose with the indignation of it all. "And while we were dealing with foreign enemies, this stripling, this callow pretender to the throne, was manipulating his hireling killers, who performed the dastardly deed for him. And now the President of Vice has taken the true President off to some dank dungeon for possible execution or some worse fate."

"I see it, but I don't believe it," Remo said in a low voice.

"Believe it. Sony would not lie."

"He's gotta be almost as strong as us," Remo said doubtfully.

"Not if he must use mere tools to work his wicked will," Chiun countered. "Sinanju has not employed implements of destruction in generations."

"I never heard of killing someone with a golf club."

"There is no limit to what certain persons will

stoop to in the unholy quest for ill-gotten glory," Chiun said sagely. "We must hasten back to America to warn Smith. No doubt the treacherous President of Vice is even now preparing to assume the Eagle Throne."

"No," Remo said as the tape ended. He popped the cassette from the camcorder. "We gotta find the President. He can't have gotten far."

A sudden voice came from the open door.

"Who could not have gotten far?"

Remo's hand shot behind his back, concealing the cassette.

"Whoever did this," he told Federal Judicial Police Officer Guadalupe Mazatl without skipping a beat. Beside him, Chiun's hands joined within his scarlet kimono sleeves.

Guadalupe Mazatl stepped into the shack.

"I do not understand this," she said, indicating the stiffening terrorists with a toss of her short hair. "Who are these *pistoleros?*"

"Terrorists," Remo said. "From the Middle East. Looks like they were the ones who knocked down *Air Force One.*"

"How did you know to come here?" Guadalupe asked suspiciously.

"Hunch," Remo said evasively.

"Because we are who we are," Chiun said in the same breath.

"And who are you really? CIA?"

"Maybe," Remo admitted because it was far enough away from the truth to be comfortable.

"And what have you behind your back?"

Remo's hand came around. Empty. The cassette nestled in the waistband of his chinos. "Nothing. I had an itch." He grinned faintly.

"To another dog with that bone," Guadalupe said disdainfully.

"What?"

"It is an expression," she said. "And I believe you know what it means."

"Not me," Remo said honestly.

"We must report this matter," Guadalupe Mazatl said.

"Fine," Remo said. "Go ahead. We'll just wait here."

Officer Guadalupe Mazatl did not move.

"I do not trust you *yanquis*. You are op to something."

"Who, us? Op to what?" Remo forced a light tone, but the anxiousness in his voice came through like a drill.

"I am not leaving without you," Officer Mazatl said firmly.

Remo looked to Chiun. Chiun looked back. Their expressions matched like red and green socks.

"Look, maybe I can level with you," Remo ventured.

"Remo," Chiun warned. "She is not to be trusted."

"Hah! Who said that of me?" Guadalupe demanded hotly.

"Comandante Odio," Chiun returned smugly.

"That *puerco!* Everyone knows that the DFS is corrupt."

"Funny, they say that about you Federales," Remo retorted.

"It is not true!" Guadalupe flared. "Of me!" she added in a metallic tone.

"Time's getting away from us here," Remo said quickly. "Listen, we have reason to believe these are some of the men responsible for shooting down the President's plane. You get word back to the others.

Tell them to be on the lookout for . . ." Remo's voice
trailed off as he realized what he was about to say.
His eyes went to the putter sticking up from one
terrorist's shattered skull.

"Sí?"

"Anyone suspicious," Remo added carefully. "Have
them scour every mountain. Extend the search area.
If there are others, they're probably on foot. They
couldn't have gotten far."

"You cannot get far on foot either."

"That's our problem," Remo shot back. "Not yours.
We're outta here. Come on, Little Father."

Officer Guadalupe Mazatl followed them outside.

"Those *gringos* are op to something," she muttered
as she watched them sprint away.

Then, clutching her pistol in its side holster, she
began running back to the crash site, pacing herself
so that she did not run out of breath.

10

The chief of staff met with the other Cabinet members in the White House conference room.

"Gentlemen, you all know the situation. Our President is no longer with us."

No one spoke a word. Their faces were gloomy.

The chief of staff went on. "Technically, the Vice-President is our new chief executive."

To a man, their faces drained of color. They looked like unhappy corpses.

"Has he taken the oath yet?" asked the Secretary of Defense uncomfortably.

"He has no inkling what has transpired."

"Wish we could keep it that way . . ." someone muttered.

"At this moment, *Air Force Two* is taking him to a Detroit location, where he will deliver a prepared speech. He knows this speech is important, but he does not know its contents. His handlers don't even know."

"Does it matter?"

"It matters very, very much," said the chief of staff. "I have had the staff prepare a speech in which the Vice-President immediately tenders his resignation for health reasons."

A husky gasp raced around the conference table.

The chief of staff silenced it with a raised hand. "I believe he can be persuaded to give this speech on one condition."

"What is that?"

"That he believes it is the President's wish that he resign."

"My God, you're talking about a palace coup!"

"No," the chief of staff countered. "I am talking about a necessary political preemptive strike. The Vice-President resigns. Then and only then do he and the nation learn that the President has died."

"But consider the political firestorm."

"Imagine, worse still, the Vice President taking his rightful place at the head of this table."

"But the next in line is what's-his-name—the Speaker of the House—a Democrat."

"I can't help that. You all know the Vice-President. He can't chew gum and walk at the same time."

"Hell, we lived through one of those presidencies back in the seventies. And the VP's a much better golfer than that guy was. At least the Vice-President never brained anyone with *his* nine-iron."

The Secretary of Housing gave a nervous little laugh. It came out like a giggle. He swallowed it.

"Gentlemen, if you have any arguments that might persuade me not to put this plan into operation, give them now. Just remember that your party is your party, but we're considering the future of America. Can the ship of state navigate these uncertain times with such an unseasoned man at the helm?"

The Cabinet exchanged unhappy, sick-eyed glances. They talked among themselves in low, urgent tones.

The chief of staff waited, his fingers steepled. He knew their decision even if they did not as yet. It was the only decision that could be made. Once again he rued the day the President had made his choice of a running mate without consultation. If only he had picked one of the other aspirants.

The decision was reached and the chief of staff looked up from his grim thoughts.

"Do what you have to," he was told.

"Thank you, gentlemen. I would join you in a prayer at this time, but every moment counts. Feel free to go ahead without me."

And as the chief of staff left the room, the remaining Cabinet members folded their hands and closed their eyes. Their lips moved, but no audible words came forth.

11

Federal Judicial Officer Guadalupe Mazatl strode across the flat sierra, her broad face a copper mask of resentment.

Overhead, the helicopters were clattering like tiny Erector Set dragonflies. The sight of their Estados Unidos insignia made her blood boil.

She did not hate the *norteamericanos*. She merely resented them, just as she resented the *criollos* who had subjugated her Indian ancestors four hundred years ago under Cortez and his mad dogs. No, she despised the *criollos*, who considered themselves more Mexican than the pure-blooded Indians, even though they were Spanish.

Glancing back over her fawn-colored shoulder, she saw the *gringo* and the old Asian he called *papacito*—"Little Father"—moving through the twisted, tortured cacti like the almighty lords of the desolation.

And as much as she despised the *criollos*, they had already done their damage. That was in the past. The *norteamericanos* threatened *mañana*.

She hurried back to the crash site to speak with the arrogant *criollo*, Comandante Odio. More was happening under the hot Mexican sun than an American airplane accident.

*　*　*

Remo Williams' eyes read the flat sierra like an open book.

The winds had disturbed the sand little. It was dark, hard-packed stuff, retaining footprints in shallows, but not in the flat crusty stretches where rainwater had stiffened the sand.

"Two men," Remo said, his eyes on the broken ground as he walked.

"Yes," Chiun said. "But one walking strangely."

"Maybe the President," Remo muttered, looking up toward the nearby mountains. "Wounded."

The Master of Sinanju shook his frail old head. "He walks heavily, but not from injury. He walks with heavy tread. As if grossly fat."

"I wondered about that," Remo said. "I thought mabye he was wearing heavy boots or something."

"Boots made of lead might leave such marks," Chiun intoned.

"Doesn't make sense," Remo said. "Let's just see where they lead us."

They led into a passage cut between two towering mountains, where ancient and rusted railroad tracks followed sun-bleached ties.

"Footprints stop here," said Remo. "See how the toes dig in, then vanish? He hopped the train."

The Master of Sinanju placed one delicate ear to a rusty rail.

"Anything?" Remo asked, looking down the tracks, which converged at the horizon line.

"There is no vibration," Chiun intoned. "The train passed some time ago."

"Well, we got something," Remo said as Chiun stood up and looked back toward the crash site. "Now all we have to do is find out where that train went, without tipping our hand."

"We should inform Smith."

"You carrying a telephone up one sleeve?"

"Of course not," bristled the Master of Sinanju.

"Then finding a phone has to be step one. Let's get back to the site."

They had covered most of the distance back to the blue-and-white broken-backed bird that had been *Air Force One* when a Mexican Army helicopter suddenly lifted up and roared toward them.

Inside the helicopter, Comandante Oscar Odio smiled broadly beneath his mirrored sunglasses.

"You will be very wise to keep silent," he told FJP Officer Mazatl. "These matters must be handled with diplomacy. I will do all the talking, *mestiza*."

"I am no mongrel *mestiza*!" Officer Mazatl spat. "I am pure *azteca*."

"Still, you will remain silent." He patted her knee. "And I would not be so proud of ancestors who cut the hearts out of the living, thinking their blood fueled the sun."

"The blood of the Inquisition was no less red," Guadalupe retorted.

Comandante Oscar Odio only laughed.

He set the helicopter down in the path of the approaching Americans.

"*Hola!*" he called through the open bubble. "*Qué pasa?*"

Remo came up first.

"Look," he shouted over the rotor whir. "I've got no time to go into details. We need to get to a phone. Pronto!"

"Your Secret Service have—how you say—ceyular *teléfonos* at the crash zone."

Remo shook his head vigorously. "No. I don't want them in on this."

"Ah," said Comandante Odio. "It is *mucho* top-secret, no?"

"Just give me a lift back to your base, okay?"

"At once," Comandante Odio said as the two climbed aboard.

The helicopter lifted up at an angle, the big rotor blade tipping in the direction they were traveling, like a buzz saw chewing through the dry air.

"Officer Mazatl tells me you have found a shack," Odio said nonchalantly.

"That's right," Remo said woodenly.

"And there were dead men in this shack."

"Right again," Remo said, looking down at the ground.

"Is there anything you would like to tell me about this matter?" Odio said good-naturedly.

"No." Remo folded his arms stubbornly.

FJP Officer Guadalupe Mazatl clentched her strong teeth. This was Mexico, not Texas. Who did these *gringos* think they were?

Then the old one spoke up.

"Where do these lead?" he asked, pointing to the railroad tracks below.

Comandante Odio glanced down.

"That is the Central route to Mexico City," he offered. "They call the train El Águila Azteca—the Aztec Eagle. Despite the name, it is a very slow train. In Mexico, everything runs slowly—*comprende?*"

"Except helicopters, I hope," Remo put in.

Taking the hint, Comandante Odio shut up. He concentrated on his flying. He felt the burning gaze of Officer Mazatl boring into him. He could also read the brown Indian woman's mind. She was thinking: How dare you let these *gringos* push you around in your own land?

He bestowed on her a dazzling smile, causing her to look away in abrupt anger.

Twenty minutes later, Comandante Oscar Odio was turning the full radiance of his Latin smile on Remo and Chiun as he escorted them into his simple office.

"Yentlemen, *mi oficina es su oficina*, as we Mexicans say."

"Thanks," Remo said brusquely, grabbing up the telephone.

"The switchboard operator will connect you to a U.S. operator," Comandante Odio added, closing the door behind him.

Fortunately for Remo, the operator spoke English. Remo gave the U.S. operator the number of a fictitious comic-book company in New York City, which relayed the call automatically to the office of Dr. Harold W. Smith on an untappable line.

While Remo listened to the line buzz, the Master of Sinanju spoke up.

"Do not forget to tell Emperor Smith that I had deduced the terrible truth before we found proof of the Vice-President's perfidy," he hissed.

The line clicked. Remo waved Chiun away.

"Smith, Remo. The President isn't dead."

"What!"

"We don't have him, but we think we know where he's heading."

"Is your line secure?" Smith asked suddenly.

"Screw security," Remo snapped. "Do you want to know about the President or don't you? I've had it with bureaucratic bullshit. We're talking about our President!"

Smith subsided. "Go ahead, Remo," he said in a sober voice.

"We followed some tracks to a little shack in the middle of nowhere," Remo explained quickly. "Found three dead terrorists there. Middle Easterners. Probably Palestinian. They had the President, but he went off with someone else."

"Who?"

Remo took a deep breath. "This is going to be hard to believe."

"Go ahead, Remo."

"Do you know where the Vice-President is right at this minute?" Remo asked in an odd voice.

"As a matter of fact, yes. They've got him on a photo opportunity tour at a drug-rehabilitation center. It's part of the White House's plan to keep him occupied until we have definite word of the President's fate."

"Well," Remo said, "sometime in the last ten hours, he was here in Mexico. He rescued the President from the terrorists."

"No!" Chiun broke in. "Remo, you are telling it wrong. The President of Vice is a conspirator. He merely dispatched his unnecessary underlings after they did his will and abducted the unfortunate President."

Remo clapped one hand over the receiver. "Let me tell it, will you, Chiun?"

"What's this?" Smith asked, his voice twisted with concern.

"At the shack we found a videotape of the abduction," Remo explained. "The President was carried from the wreckage alive. The terrorists were filming him inside this shack when the Vice-President burst in swinging—I know how this sounds—golf clubs. He took the terrorists apart. It was a massacre."

"The Vice-President of the United States?" Smith asked doubtfully.

"No," Remo shot back sarcastically. "The Vice-President of Exxon. I've got the tape to prove it, too."

"Remo," Smith said firmly, "the Vice-President was awakened this morning in his own bed, by his own handlers and at the request of the White House, and bundled off to this drug-rehabilitation-center appearance."

"Are you sure he's the real Vice-President?" Remo asked.

"How do you know the man on the tape is?" Smith countered.

"Looks like him, right down to the golf swing."

"The Vice-President would never plot against the country."

"No? Remember that stock-market thing we dealt with a few months back? And the secret English descendants infrastructure that was dedicated to selling the US out to Great Britain? The Vice-President was on the list of secret British loyalists."

"That threat has been terminated. I cannot believe the Vice-President would act to undermine this country."

"Well, something's screwy down here. Look, we think they hopped a train to Mexico City."

"Then go to Mexico City. But keep this to yourself."

"From my lips to God's ears," Remo said, hanging up.

In the next room, Comandante Oscar Odio waited for the extension receiver to click before he hung up. His face wore an uncharacteristic frown. It was astonishing, what he had overheard. The American Vice-President in Mexico? A coup underway in the United States?

But most intriguing was the intelligence that the President himself was not dead, but alive somewhere in Mexico. It was very, very valuable information to a man who knew how to disseminate such things correctly.

He left the room of his secretary and rejoined Officer Mazatl in the hall outside his own office. Mazatl stood there, her brown thumb hooked into her black belt like some *caballero de pulquería*. She did not at all resemble a woman, Odio thought.

Nevertheless, he smiled at her pleasantly. The smile was not returned. If anything, Mazatl's obsidian eyes grew harder.

"If you would like to use the men's room, Officer, it is down the hall." His smile didn't waver as he delivered the insult.

"*Hijo de la chingada!*" Mazatl spat venomously.

The *comandante* only laughed. He grew sincere when the *americanos* stepped into the hall.

"We've got to get back to our embassy," the one called Remo said urgently.

"By all means," Comandante Odio said. "I understand *perfectamente*. Please accept my condolences on the loss of your beloved *presidente*," he added sorrowfully.

"Thanks," Remo said distantly.

"And," Comandante Odio added, "as a gesture of solidarity with you in your bereavement, please allow Officer Mazatl to escort you back to Mexico City."

Officer Mazatl whirled.

"I am not under your command!" she spat.

"Of course not, *señorita*," Odio said oilily. "But I am certain your superiors would want you to see that the American diplomats are well taken care of. You would not want them to become lost in our very large country."

"We can take care of ourselves," Remo said flatly.

"But the officer will expedite your trip," Odio insisted. "I am certain you do not wish to wait for a Mexicana flight, since they often meet with unfortunate delays. I will arrange military transportation for you."

"Okay," Remo relented, "but only because we're in a rush."

Odio turned to Officer Mazatl. He smiled. "*Señorita?*"

"I will go with these two," she said sullenly, "but not because you expect it."

"As you wish, Officer Mazatl."

The *comandante* departed to make the arrangements.

FJP Officer Mazatl stepped up to Remo and Chiun. She looked Remo hard in the eyes.

"You are concealing something," she hissed. "I can tell that."

"Prove it," said Remo, feeling the hard edge of the videotape in the small of his back.

12

Jorge Chingar sat beside his telephone in his palatial hacienda outside the Colombian town of Cali. All morning long the calls kept coming in.

"Padrino, the U.S. President has not yet arrived."

"Padrino, still no sign of *Air Force Uno*."

"Padrino, the other conference representatives are beginning to wonder what is keeping the *presidente*."

All morning long. But no concrete word on the U.S. President's fate. It was maddening. His spies in Bogotá faithfully updated him every half-hour. But there was yet no word from his Palestinian compadres. Surely they would have called by this time. Perhaps they had been captured in Mexico. It was a pleasant thought. Death to the American President, and Jorge Chingar could keep the money promised for the deed. The Palestinians were fools of a sort, after all. No one else in their business would have undertaken such a daring task without first obtaining a substantial down payment.

But these men had been so eager to make their reputation that all that seemed to matter was getting the job.

Jorge Chingar, known as El Padrino—"The God-

father"—already had a reputation. He also had a
million-dollar estate outside of Bogatá—until the
Colombian Army, backed up by U.S. DEA agents,
swooped down upon it in the middle of the night,
forcing El Padrino to flee into the hot jungle wearing
only his silk underwear.

He was not without resources, principally caches
of money and armaments. It had been a simple enough
matter to set up again in a safe house, one unknown
to the Colombian government.

But the indignity of it offended El Padrino and he
had sworn, even as his bare feet slipped on the wet
jungle grasses that evil night, that he would make
the President of the United States pay.

The phone rang again. He grabbed it with his
many-ringed right hand.

"*Sí?*"

"El Padrino?"

"*Sí.*"

"This is Comandante Odio. From the Mexican DFS.
We have done business before."

"Of course. How may I be of service to you,
comandante?"

"Ah," said the smiling voice. "You are mistaken. It
is how I may be of service to *you.*"

"Go on. I am listening."

"Your hatred of the American *presidente* is not
unknown to me. I thought you might be interested
in knowing that *Air Force One* crashed in the Sierra
Madres last night."

"Ah!" said El Padrino with only a slight lifting of
his voice. "This interests me. Pray, go on."

"The Americans have secured the crash site. They
believe their *presidente* is dead."

"*Muy malo,*" chuckled El Padrino.

"They cannot find the body."

"*Muy triste,*" El Padrino said with mock sadness.

"But I happen to know that the President is very much alive."

El Padrino snapped to attention. "*Qué?* How you know this? Tell me!"

"He has been taken to Mexico City, apparently by the Vice-President, his subordinate. I do not understand it myself, but even now there is a coup under way in Washington."

"A coup?"

"Engineered by the Vice-President, Padrino."

"Preposterous."

"I have this on excellent authority. *Impeccable* authority."

"What does the Vice-President intend to do with the President?"

"I do not know, Padrino."

"I would like to know. And I would pay exceedingly well the man who brings me such information—or proof that the *presidente* is dead. *Comprende?*"

"I will contact you directly that I have good news for you, Padrino," Comandante Oscar Odio said briskly. "*Adiós.*"

"*Vaya con Dios,*" said El Padrino, replacing the receiver. He snapped his fingers twice and a hulking bodyguard stepped in from the next room.

"Pollo," he commanded. "Gather your best *pistoleros*. You are going to Mexico City. There is someone I would like you to kill there."

"*Sí*, Padrino."

13

It was the most miserable ride in the President's memory.

Going down in flames in the South Pacific during World War II had been no moonlight cruise, to be sure. But except for some bad moments bobbing in the water, it had been over quick.

The train ride through the brown desolation of rural Mexico seemed to go on forever, and nothing he said to the Vice-President, no plea, no veiled threat, could persuade him to enter the caboose.

"But I'm the President," he muttered, his teeth rattling like castanets. The springs on the caboose were either old or sprung. If it even had springs. "This is a friendly country, real friendly. People down here know my face. Hell, I got grandchildren who are Mexican."

The Vice-President turned his perpetually wounded eyes on him like blue lasers. "My prime directive is survival. Entering the train is not conducive to our survival. Must survive. Must ensure your survival. Your survival will ensure my survival. My survival will guarantee your survival. Our survival—"

"I getcha," chattered the President. The poor guy

was still rattled. He'd been going on and on about survival like a tape-message loop. "But if I don't have some water soon, I don't know if I'm gonna survive."

That got a reaction. "Wait here. I will get water."

And the Vice-President came to his feet like his knees had sprung. He clambered up an attached ladder to the caboose roof and disappeared. Over the clickety-clack of the rails, the President heard his feet clump away heavily.

"Amazing!" the President said, his newfound awe of his Vice-President swelling. "When this is over, I'm gonna put that guy up for a Congressional Medal of Honor. And screw those jerks who called him a draft dodger."

The President huddled at the metal railing of the caboose platform. He clung to it with one hand, fearful of falling off. It was warm. Not hot. The sun was high and eye-stingingly bright, but he could stand it. The wind cut through his poplin windbreaker relentlessly.

The Vice-President came down the caboose carrying a plastic cup. He offered it, saying, "I found this."

"Thanks," the President said, taking quick gulps. The water tasted good. "Want some?"

"No. I do not need water."

"Great," said the President, who really hadn't wanted to share in the first place. He drained the cup.

"Damn! That was good. Wish I had more."

"I will provide more water," the Vice-President said. "Water is important for your survival."

"No, no," the President said quickly. "Stay put.

No sense risking your neck again running along the train top."

"I will not need to do that. I now carry a reserve supply."

The Vice-President took the plastic glass, and turning his back on the President, did something with it. The President's brow wrinkled at the sound of gurgling water. He sneaked a look. The Vice-President held one hand over the glass. He thought he saw water dribbling off the man's fingertips.

The glass came back into his hand, and the President took a tentative sip. He made a face.

"Tastes oily," he said.

"It will not harm you. Nothing will harm you while I am with you. It is important that you know that."

"Know it?" the President said, draining the glass in quick gulps. "I'm gonna see that you get the best thank-you note ever written. The very best. What do you think of that?"

"The job of protecting you is a job," the Vice-President said blankly.

"Great, Dan," the President said with concern. "Could I ask you why you've got that smile on your face?"

"This is the smile that is always on the face of the Vice-President."

"Yeah, true. But not like that. It looks kinda . . . fixed. You're starting to remind me of that Joker fella, from the movie. Think you could relax just a little?"

The smile dropped two stops on the register. "Is this satisfactory?" the Vice-President asked.

"Better," the President admitted.

The smiled dropped another stop, with German lens precision.

"Is this best?"

"Good. Yeah, keep it like that."

I gotta make sure this guy gets a full psychiatric evaluation at Walter Reed, the President thought. He's acting loopier than ever.

"We are nearing a city," the Vice-President said as the mountains grew thinner around them.

"How do you know that?"

"I can smell the pollution. It is very dense. There are harmful elements in the air—sulfur dioxides, carbon monoxide, zinc particles, and fecal dust."

"Must be Mexico City," the President said, suddenly impressed by his Vice-President's keen sense of smell. "I understand on really bad days the birds actually drop out of the sky from the smog. Imagine that. Hey, we have an embassy in Mexico City. We'll go there."

"Will they assist our survival?"

"Damn right. They'll assure it."

"Then we will go there."

"Of course we will," the President said, sticking his hands between his thighs for warmth.

The train began to slow and shacks appeared on either side. They looked miserable, like something found on the outskirts of a war-torn third-world battle zone. The President had traveled through Mexico before, but had never seen the rural part up close like this. It was difficult to imagine that this kind of squalor existed only a few hundred miles below the Texas border.

A road appeared on the left, and as the train slowed, the road came closer and closer to the railbed until the train and the sparse traffic were running parallel to one another.

"Someone's gonna see us," the President warned.

"I will protect you."

"Glad to hear it, but that's not what I meant. Maybe they'll recognize us. Help us out."

A dull gray truck with a wooden flatbed rumbled past the train, going in the opposite direction. The President noticed it because the back was crowded with a dozen or more men standing up. As they zoomed by, they reacted with shouts and pointing fingers.

The truck executed a fumy U-turn and came up alongside the caboose. The men surged to the near side of the truck bed. One waved and shouted, "*El presidente?*"

"*Sí! Sí!*" the President answered, getting to his feet. He waved with one hand, clutching the rail with the other. "*Soy el presidente de los Estados Unidos!*"

A shout went up from the men, who wore dusty clothing. They looked like ragtag Mexican farmers.

The truck picked up speed and left them breathing its malodorous exhaust.

"They're going for help!" the President shouted joyously. "We can relax now. They must have been looking for us all along."

"They possess weapons which can harm you," the Vice-President said mechanically.

"Guns are real popular down here. It's that *machismo* thing."

The train was rounding a bend, giving the President an unobstructed view of the engine. The truck drew up alongside it. Suddenly a battery of rifles and automatic weapons came level, like a firing squad on wheels.

"Must be trying to get the attention of the engineer," the President ventured. "Fella probably can't hear them over the engine racket."

The guns opened up. The firing was intense, a rattling ineffectual *pop-pop-pop* mixed with the harsh snap of bullets bouncing off the heavy engine.

"What the hell are they doing?" the President said, ducking for cover. "That's a lot of shooting for a warning shot."

"We must escape," the Vice-President said with metallic urgency. The train was slowing down.

"For God's sake, what's going on?"

The train ground to a jerky halt and the truck came back, its human cargo shouting and caterwauling like Pancho Villa's army.

The President was no fool. He realized this was no rescue party. Before he could say, "Let's get out of here!" a firm hand took him by the waist and yanked him down behind the caboose, pushing him against a multiwheeled truck assembly.

"These wheels will protect you," he said. The Vice-President crept forward.

"Where are you going?" the President demanded anxiously.

The Vice-President did not answer. He disappeared between the couplings that joined the caboose to the rest of the train.

The President hugged his knees to his chest and tried to make himself as small as he could. He ruefully thought that whatever dangers had awaited him in Bogotá, they would be infinitely preferable to what was happening right now.

He listened to the mixture of sounds—more excited shouting, the gunning of the truck engine, and the lengthy squeal of its tires in a wild turn. They were coming back.

The truck braked nearby, and feet hit the asphalt with hard leather slaps. They were jumping off the truck, yelling exultantly.

The President sneaked a peek around a heavy steel wheel rim.

He saw many booted feet. They surrounded another pair of feet—the Vice-President's. The Vice-President seemed to hold his ground as he was surrounded. They were the bravest feet the President had ever seen.

Nothing happened for a long moment, except excited shouting and questioning. One word was repeated: *"Cabrón."* That meant "friend," the President recalled, thinking back to his high-school Spanish. No, wait—it meant "bastard," he decided, remembering his Texas oil days. They were calling the Vice-President a bastard, questioning him, but not hurting him. They repeated the words *el presidente* many times, with growing vehemence.

The President wondered if he should surrender. They might kill the Vice-President if he didn't answer—and it sounded as if he wouldn't. Brave fella.

As he was deciding, something happened. Two sets of boots suddenly left the ground. They just vanished. Then two broken bodies landed in the place where they had been. There came a scream. The President pulled his head back. He tried to make himself small again.

And the gunfire started in earnest.

Pop-pop-pop-pop-pop-pop. Like distant firecrackers.

More screams. It went on for a long time. There were other sounds—meaty twisty ripping noises. Fleeing feet. Commotion.

The President waited tensely for it all to die down. He knew better than to run when bullets were ripping the air, although his nerves screamed for him to flee.

The gun sounds were still ringing in his ears when he heard footsteps coming for him. They crushed the railbed gravel.

The President's eyes snapped open. He got ready to duck under the caboose.

To his astonishment, the Vice-President—his eyes still holding that perpetual hurt light that never changed from debate to photo op, his clown grin almost ghoulish in its unwavering fixity—stepped into view.

"We are safe now," he said, reaching down. "We have survived." He held a bent putter in his other hand.

The President let himself be helped to his feet. His ankles and knees felt like Slinky toys waggling in opposite directions.

"What happened?" he asked shakily.

"The meat machines have been neutralized."

"Meat machines?" the President asked. Steadying himself against the caboose, he peered around to the other side.

He gagged. For he could see why the Vice-President had called their erstwhile attackers meat machines. They had been torn limb from limb. The fortunate ones. Their ham-bone joints gleamed white at the torn-off shoulders and knees.

The President threw up his water. The Vice-President straightened the putter's shaft with a quick two-handed motion and restored it to his bag.

"You did all that what a putter?" the President said incredulously.

"Yes. Why?"

The question was asked with such a straight face that all the President could do was mutter, "Well, not much loft in a putter." He felt very weak. "I don't think I can go on," he said.

"We must survive," said the Vice-President.

"Amen," said the President fervently.

"I will carry you."

"No, no—you've done enough."

But the Vice-President was having none of it. Like a caveman, he took the chief executive around the waist and hefted him onto his hip like a feather pillow.

"This isn't really necessary."

The Vice-President stepped out into the road and started walking with a steady metronomic gait.

"Isn't there a more dignified way to do this?" the President wanted to know as he bounced on the Vice-President's anvil hip.

"You are too weak to walk. I am strong. I am very strong."

"Thank goodness for that. Those fellas were trying to kill us. You just took them apart."

"Yes. We cannot go to the embassy now. We must enter the city undetected if we are to survive."

"How are we gonna do that?"

"I will find a way," the Vice-President said. "We must seek sanctuary."

"Let's find one with food. I'm getting hungry."

"What would you like?"

"Anything."

The Vice-President's camera-lens eyes regarded an approaching truck. "Bread?" he asked.

"Sure. Anything. Even plain white bread would taste good."

No sooner were the words out of the President's mouth than he was set onto the roadside. His head no longer hanging upside down over the concrete, he looked around him.

The train was not far behind. It stood there like a long inert worm of metal. Passengers' screams were more audible, but no one had ventured from the cars.

The Vice-President stepped into the middle of the road, his arms raised. He was trying to flag down a blue-and-white van coming up the road.

The van stopped and the Vice-President stepped up to the driver's side. The driver rolled down the window and asked, *"Como está?"*

Without warning, the Vice-President delivered a straight-arm punch. The driver's head slumped out the window, unconscious.

When the Vice-President came back for him, he was wearing that idiot Alfred E. Neuman grin of his, as if nothing had happened.

"Did you have to hit him like that?" the President complained.

"I did not speak his language, and we can trust no one," the Vice-President said, and under his arm went the President again. He was bundled into the back of the van. The door slammed and darkness closed over him.

"Hey!" the President shouted.

"Enjoy your meal," said the Vice-President's voice.

The truck started up. It rattled worse than the caboose.

The President became aware of the tantalizing smell of fresh bread. On one hand and both knees, he felt around in the back, encountering plastic wrapping on shelves upon shelves of plastic wrapping.

He tore one open and began to devour handfuls of soft aeirated bread. It tasted like Wonder Bread. It would have tasted better, but the awful exhaust smell was coming up through the floorboards. Still, it was good to eat solid food again.

After he had filled his stomach, drowsiness set in. The President fell promptly asleep. His last loggy thought was to wonder what had come over the Vice-President. The guy had become a positive tiger.

14

The plane that ferried Remo and Chiun to Mexico City International Airport was a rickety propeller-driven Douglas C-47 of museum vintage.

After a long period of silence—among the three passengers, but not the rattling cabin—Remo commented on that fact.

"How is it your helicopters are so modern, but your planes belong in the junkyard?"

"Do you insult my country's military?" Guadalupe Mazatl demanded hotly.

"Just wondering," Remo said, folding his bare arms. He wasn't in the mood for conversation anyway. Not with Chiun, who felt that as long as no blame fell on his shoulders, it didn't matter what happened to the President of the United States, and especially not with a sullen Mexican cop with a chip on her shoulder almost as large as her inferiority complex.

The ground below was endlessly mountainous. Remo wondered if all of Mexico was this barren.

"The helicopter, it belonged to him."

"What's that?" Remo asked, roused from his thoughts by Guadalupe's sullen voice.

"That was Comandante Odio's private helicopter. I

have heard that he bought it himself and merely
lends it to his command."

"They must pay DFS commandants pretty well
down here," Remo remarked.

"They do not," Guadalupe Mazatl said flatly.

Remo's eyebrows shot up. "You suggesting the
comandante is on the take?"

"I suggest nothing. You are a smart *norteamericano*.
You put *dos* and *dos* together."

"Two and two."

"I said that."

"Well," Remo returned, "he was very helpful to
us."

"He is not a man worthy of trust."

"Not my problem. I'll never see him again."

"Then I trust you said nothing during your telephone conversation that you would not want him to
know."

Remo eyed Guadalupe's masklike profile. "Why is
that?"

"He was undoubtedly listening in on your call."

"How do you know that?" the Master of Sinanju
said, taking interest in the conversation for the first
time.

"He left me alone in the hall," Guadalupe explained.

"Circumstantial," Remo suggested.

"And he can afford a modern helicopter on less
than three hundred pesos salary per month."

Remo looked across the aisle to the Master of
Sinanju.

"What do you think, Little Father?" he asked.

"I think I will be happy when I am out of this
wounded metal bird."

"You're a big help. By the way," he asked Guadalupe, "what do they call you for short? Guad?"

"Lupe."

"Loopy," Remo said. "Doesn't fit you, you know."

The plane set down at Mexico City International Airport and ground personnel rolled out an aluminum stairway so they could deplane.

"I gotta find a phone," Remo told Lupe as they stepped onto the tarmac.

"Come with me."

They entered the busy terminal and FJP Officer Mazatl found the operations manager. After exchanging swift words with him in Spanish, she led him from the office, telling Remo, "We will be outside."

"Listening in?" Remo asked. But he smiled when he said it. His smile was not returned.

"Let's see what Smith has to say," Remo told Chiun.

"I do not like this place," Chiun said suddenly while Remo waited for a U.S. operator to come on the line.

"Already? We haven't even left the airport."

"This is an evil place," Chiun insisted. "The air tastes like metal."

"I did notice the sky was kinda brown, at that," Remo remarked. Then, into the phone: "Smith? Remo. We're in Mexico City. Any news? . . . Really? . . . Here? Well, it's a lead. No word on the President? . . . I see. . . . Okay. We'll register at a hotel. I have a police escort I'll need to ditch, but that shouldn't be a problem. Her nickname is Loopy."

Remo hung up.

"Smith says there was a report that the Vice-President was seen in Mexico City only an hour ago," he told Chiun.

"You see!" Chiun said triumphantly. "Proof of all I said. What dastardly crime has he committed now?"

"He was seen driving a bread truck through the city."

"Perhaps the bread is poisoned," Chiun said as he followed Remo from the office.

"We've got to get to the embassy," Remo informed Lupe.

"I will drive you," she said.

"Thanks, but no thanks. Just call us a cab."

"I am your host and protector while you are in Mexico," Lupe said stiffly.

"Thanks again, but we don't need protection."

Lupe's hard eyes flicked toward the Master of Sinanju. "The old one. He looks pale."

"Don't let that fool you," Remo retorted. "He's healthier than I am. Right, Chiun?"

The Master of Sinanju said nothing. He sniffed the air with concern.

Remo looked more closely. "You *do* look a little pale, at that."

"I do not like this place," Chiun said again.

"Fine," Remo returned. "Let's be on our way."

Officer Guadalupe Mazatl led them out to the drop-off area, where she flagged a cab.

"No official vehicle?" Remo asked as they got in.

"An FJP jeep might arrive in five minutes or five hours. This taxi is here now."

They pulled into traffic a moment later, and were soon traveling through a rundown area of scabrous stucco buildings; there was a general air of forlorn hopelessness about the people walking along the streets.

Remo kept an eye on the traffic, looking for bread

trucks. Smith had told him the brand name. What was it again?

"You ever heard of Bimbo Bread?" he asked Lupe suddenly.

Sí. It is a well-known brand here in the Distrito Federal. Why?"

"Oh, nothing," Remo said evasively.

They turned on an artery called Viaducto. Remo wondered if it was Spanish for "viaduct," and if it was, why it was called that.

After a while the avenue sank into the ground and their view of the city was cut off by ugly gray concrete walls lifting on either side, like a viaduct that carried traffic instead of water.

The city was incredibly congested, Remo saw. Noxious exhaust poured from the tailpipe of every car and truck. It was worse than New York or L.A. But there was something different about it, too.

As they turned off Viaducto, under a huge electric pinwheel of a sign—"TOME COCA-COLA"—back into ground-level traffic, a blue VW Beetle slithered out of their way, causing a chain reaction of near-collisions.

Their cabdriver kept going as if this were an everyday occurrence. Remo looked back. Miraculously, no one was hurt. Then it hit him.

"Don't the cars have horns down here?"

"*Sí*," Lupe said. "Why do you ask?"

"In New York, you'd hear a million car horns during a near-disaster like that."

A faint smile touched the corners of Lupe's lips.

"Perhaps we are more civilized in Mexico than you would think," she said.

"Matter of fact," Remo added, "I don't hear *any* horns. It's unnatural."

The cabdriver spoke up. "Many drivers, *señor*, they carry *pistolas*."

"So much for civilization," Remo said smugly.

Lupe Mazatl said nothing. In the front seat, beside the driver, the Master of Sinanju was equally silent.

Remo looked around for trucks. He saw none that said "Bimbo Bread." Then he realized that it might not say "bread" at all.

"What's the Spanish for 'bread'?" he asked Lupe.

"*Pan.*"

"How about 'bimbo'?"

" 'Bimbo'?"

"Yeah. 'Bimbo.' What's that in English?"

Lupe shrugged her uniformed shoulders. " 'Bimbo' is . . . 'bimbo.' "

"In the U.S. a bimbo is a girl who's not very bright."

Lupe's brown forehead puckered. "She is dark?"

"No, unintelligent. Dumb. You know, stupid."

"Ah, *señorita estúpida*. 'Stupid girl.' That is what you wish to know?"

"Maybe," Remo said, frowning. He didn't think that anyone would invent a brand name that meant "stupid girl." Maybe Lupe was right. Maybe "bimbo" was just "bimbo." He decided on another tack.

"What color are the Bimbo Bread trucks down here?"

A dark notch formed between Guadalupe's thick brows.

"Why this concern with Bimbo Bread?" she asked suspiciously.

"Nothing special," Remo said innocently. "Just trying to soak up local customs."

"Why do you not ask about our fine culture, then?

Our great city? Do you know that Mexico City is the most populous in the world?"

"I can believe it," Remo said, looking out at the congestion. They were stopped at an intersection where a traffic cop in a chocolate-and-cream uniform was attempting to unsnarl traffic with a white baton. It looked hopeless. The red "ALTO" signs were being ignored in both directions.

"We have the longest avenue in the world here in Mexico City," Lupe said proudly. "It is called the Avenida Insurgentes. And our Chapultepec Park is unrivaled for its magnificence."

"Skip the tourist-brochure stuff," Remo said. "I'm already here."

When they got going again, Remo noticed that the Master of Sinanju was staring out the window, his face a frown of wrinkles, like a parchment death mask left too long in the sun.

"You've been awful quiet, Little Father," he said solicitously.

"I have a headache," Chiun's voice was muted.

"You!" Remo said aghast, and the shock in his face was not lost on Guadalupe Mazatl.

"Is this serious?" she asked.

"Is it?" Remo asked Chiun solicitously.

"This is a foul place," Chiun said brittlely. "I have a headache and my breathing rhythms are not properly centered."

"Does it hurt behind the eyes?" Lupe asked.

Chiun turned. "Yes. What do you know of this?"

"It is a pollution headache," Lupe explained. "Many *turistas* get these things. They are not used to the thin air or the smog. Our smog, I regret to say, is also famous. Mexico lies in a high valley and the mountains that surround it form a natural—how you say—cop."

"Cup, not cop," Remo said absently. He was looking at Chiun. He had never seen his teacher ill a day in his life. As old and frail as the Master of Sinanju appeared, under the wrinkles and semitranslucent skin, he was a human dynamo. "Are you going to be all right, Little Father?"

"We must leave this place as soon as we can," Chiun croaked. "The air is bad and the oxygen thinner than Tibet's."

"Soon as we accomplish our mission," Remo assured him.

"Mission?" Lupe asked.

"Did I ask you what color a Bimbo Bread truck is?" Remo said quickly.

"Sí." And you would not tell me why you thought this important."

"Forget it," Remo said. "An idle question."

"Blue," said the Master of Sinanju. "Blue and white."

Remo leaned forward. "How do you know that?"

"Because there is one in front of us."

Remo followed Chiun's pointing finger—it trembled almost imperceptibly—and saw the back of a blue-and-white bread truck. The word "Bimbo" was plainly visible, as were a loaf of bread and a fluffy white cartoon bear.

"Driver," Remo said urgently, "try to pull up on the driver's side of that truck."

"What is this?" Lupe demanded.

"Later," Remo said. "Driver, do it!"

The traffic was thick, but the driver tried. He jockeyed in and out of the traffic flow with a kind of wild precision.

At a traffic light, they pulled up alongside the truck.

Remo rolled down the window, getting a faceful of noxious warm air. He put his head out, but all he could see was a patch of sky reflected in the bread-truck driver's mirror.

"Can you see anything, Little Father?" he demanded.

The Master of Sinanju put his head out. He looked up, and Remo saw his beard hair tremble. His tiny mouth dropped open.

And before Remo could react, Chiun burst out of the car, shaking a tiny furious fist.

"You!" he shrieked. "Traitor!"

Remo started to open his door, calling, "Chiun, what are you doing?"

The bread truck surged ahead, cutting off the taxi. The Master of Sinanju leapt after it.

Remo flew out of the back and gave chase, oblivious of Guadalupe Mazatl's shouting after him.

Up ahead, the Master of Sinanju was running like an octogenarian Olympic torchbearer, fists pumping high, legs working like spindly pistons under his flopping kimono hem.

The truck veered crazily, causing near-accidents at every turn. Still, not a horn honked. Not a curse was shouted in any language. Unless one counted the excited imprecations of the Master of Sinanju as he hauled after the zigzagging truck.

Remo drew abreast of the Master of Sinanju, his own running motions controlled and tight.

"Chiun! What did you see? Who's driving?"

"The . . . puff . . . President of . . . puff . . . Vice," Chiun wheezed. His voice rattled.

"You sure?"

"I would know that callow, treacherous visage any-where!" Chiun wheezed.

"Look, you're not breathing right," Remo pleaded. "Leave this to me."

"No!" said Chiun, sprinting forward.

"Oh, great," Remo said. "Now he's got to show me up."

The Bimbo Bread truck came to a rotary of sorts, dominated by a huge white column surmounted by a gold-leaf angel. Remo grinned, knowing that the driver would have to slow down to manage the sharp curve.

But he did not slow down. With almost computer-like precision he sped into the circle and began orbiting the massive column like a satellite on wheels.

"What's he doing?" Remo muttered, falling in behind the truck. He stayed with it for one orbit. Midway through the second, he decided to cut across the monument. The noxious fumes of the exhaust were starting to make him feel whoozy.

Remo sprinted across the monument, up the shallow steps, and back down again.

He alighted on the opposite side—just in time to intercept the speeding truck.

His eyes flicked once toward the Master of Sinanju, pelting around in the truck's wake.

He saw a winded, red-faced Chiun, slowing down, his arms jerking unsynchronously, like those of a Boston Marathon runner at Heartbreak Hill, his legs wavering.

"He's in trouble," Remo muttered worriedly.

Suddenly, the Master of Sinanju stumbled, a big green *colectivo* bus only yards behind him.

Remo's eyes jumped to the approaching bread truck and went back to Chiun. The sun on the windshield obscured the driver's face.

Swearing to himself, he let the truck roar past and raced back to rescue his mentor.

The green bus was not stopping. The driver's dark eyes were fixed on the traffic, not the road. The Master of Sinanju was raising himself off the asphalt with trembling arms, his face dazed.

Remo's mind raced, making instinctual mental calculations he could not have duplicated with pen and paper. The speed of the truck, his own velocity, even the air resistance pressing against his chest. They all coalesced into some deep untranslatable knowledge.

Remo picked up speed, bent at the waist, and without pause scooped up the Master of Sinanju with bare inches between them and a big bus tire.

The bus whizzed by, sucking at the hairs at the back of Remo's head.

He deposited the Master of Sinanju on the grass of a little square park. He felt his own lungs burning slightly, as if he had somehow inhaled fire.

"Chiun! Are you all right?" he said with difficulty.

"The air is poison here!" Chiun wheezed. His eyes were closed, his thin chest heaving with each breath.

"Yeah. I'm starting to feel it too." Remo settled back. He concentrated on his own breathing. The air was heavy. He had been aware of it ever since leaving the airport, but he hadn't noticed the thin oxygen content. The pollution particles had masked that deficiency.

Now, in the strange humming drone of Mexico City traffic, he became slowly aware that his head was beginning to throb.

"This is not good," said Remo Williams, who had not had a headache or a cold or any other common minor infirmity since achieving the early states of the

art of Sinanju. "And that Lupe is probably looking
for us right now. Are you up to ditching her?"

"I am up to returning to America," Chiun said
weakly.

"Soon as we can," Remo promised. He stood up,
looking for a taxi.

He flagged down a yellow VW Beetle with black
and white checks on the doors as it came around the
circle.

"Where are the best hotels?" Remo asked the
driver. "The ones with air-conditioning."

"In the Zona Rosa, *señor*. The Pink Zone."

"Then take us to the Pink Zone," Remo said,
assisting Chiun into the back.

"Zona Rosa, *sí*," the driver said. The cab scooted
down a street and back up another. They passed
streets with European names like Hamburgo, Ge-
nova, and Copenhague.

"You feeling any better, Little Father?" Remo asked.

"I will live," Chiun said stiffly. His eyes were
closed. He looked very old all of a sudden, Remo
thought. He always looked old. But Remo had long
ago learned to trust—and respect—the power that
flowed under the wizened shell of the man who was
his teacher. He sensed that power ebbing, and it
worried him.

Sooner than Remo expected, they were tooling
down a street called Florencia, where a row of tall
palms dominated a center island. They passed trendy-
looking boutiques and even some American restaurants.

Remo was about to ask the driver why it was called
the Pink Zone when he noticed that the cobbled
sidewalks were faintly pink from paint that had been
worn thin by rain and the tread of countless feet.

Abruptly the driver pulled up to a corner. He turned around, saying, "Two hundred pesos, *señor*."

"How do you know this is where I want to get off?"

The driver shrugged, muttering something Remo didn't catch.

"What did he say, Chiun?"

The Master of Sinanju put the same question to the driver, and translated the reply.

"He said, 'This is a good place to get off,' " Chiun explained.

"Why not?" Remo said, getting out. He paid the driver in coins, knowing he was overtipping but not caring. He was sick of the heavy Mexican money rattling in his pockets. It all came out of his CURE operating expenses anyway.

The cab pulled away. Remo looked around. He was standing before a boutique called Banana. The roof had been done over to resemble Jungleland. A giant version of King Kong clutched a hairless mannequin against the backdrop of papier-mâché trees.

"Let's find a hotel," Remo said, stepping around the corner onto a street called Liverpool.

The first hotel he came to was in an area dotted with earthquake-shattered buildings. The glass face of the Hotel Krystal was undamaged.

"Looks fine to me," Remo said. "So long as the earth doesn't move."

They checked in and, once in the air-conditioned room, began to feel less light-headed. Remo poured out the contents of a bottle of complimentary purified water into two glasses and gave one to the Master of Sinanju. That helped too.

Chiun sat up in one of the big beds.

"I recognized the President of Vice, Remo."

"No kidding," Remo said dryly, looking out at the Mexican skyline. It was magnificently broad and seemed to extend as far as the ring of distant mountains. The sky was darkening to a steely elemental color, as if it was about to rain toxic metals.

"But there is something else," Chiun added.

"Yeah?"

"He recognized me. That is why he ran."

"Can't be. He's never seen us. He shouldn't know we exist."

"The look in his eyes told me that he recognized me," Chiun insisted. "Not in his face. It was like the mask of a clown, always grinning. But his eyes. They told me that he knew my face and feared me."

"Impossible!"

"It is so," Chiun repeated firmly.

"Look, I'm going to need you on this," Remo said anxiously. "Are you up to it, or not?"

"I will serve my emperor," the Master of Sinanju said weakly.

"I'd better call Smith."

"Tell him what I have told you."

"He's not going to believe any of this," Remo muttered, punching the telephone keypad.

15

The headquarters for CURE, the supersecret U.S. government agency that existed in no budget, employed no official staff, and yet possessed a multimillion-dollar operating budget, was a second-floor office in a sleepy private hospital in Rye, New York.

The name on the plain door was Harold W. Smith, who was officially director of the hospital, incorporated as Folcroft Sanitarium.

For nearly three decades Smith, formerly with the CIA, had helmed CURE from its early days of crisis management through times of grave political uncertainty. He had not been young when the even younger President had offered him the monumental task of preserving American democracy from those who would twist the Constitution to achieve their vicious ends. And he was not young now.

Smith sat in the same chair he had first occupied in the first day on the job, staring into a modest computer terminal on his desk. He looked like a man who had spent his youth locked in a dank basement eating only lemons and the occasional hard crust of bread. His skin was grayish and dry, his mouth puckered in thought. Behind the prim transparencies of his rimless eyeglasses, his eyes were gray where they should be gray and red where they should have been white.

Smith watched the message-traffic intercepts scrolling before his eyes. The White House was clamped down like a fortress. Cryptic, carefully guarded messages were going back and forth in the State Department and from there to the CIA station in Mexico City.

The lid was still on. It would not stay on long, Smith knew.

He leaned into the screen, his long patrician nose almost bumping the glare-free glass. His fingers lifted like a pianist's. The dry clicking of the keys was as close to music as lemony Harold Smith ever made.

Smith brought up the whereabouts of the Vice-President. All was calm there. He was definitely where he should be.

So whom had Remo and Chiun seen—or supposedly seen—on the Mexican videotape?

"An impostor," he muttered. "Must be." Or was it as Remo had suggested, the other way around?

There was no way Smith could verify either theory. His eyes darted to the black dialless red telephone that sat within easy reach. Normally it was his hot line to the White House. But now there was no one there to pick up the phone. Other than the President, no one in the executive branch knew of Smith or CURE or any of it. That was one of the safeguards built into CURE, which, if it was discovered, would have to be disbanded, because to admit it existed was to admit that one gray man hunched over a computer screen, unknown and unelected, as well as two of the finest assassins ever known, was all that kept America from slipping over the brink into anarchy—or worse.

Smith considered the possibility that the Vice-President had somehow been responsible for the downing of *Air Force One*. He immediately resolved not to communicate with the man until he knew for an absolute certainty that the President had been lost and the Vice-President was not complicit. He had that option. CURE was autonomous of the executive branch.

Smith switched over to the wire services and TV news digests, automatically processed by the massive computers hidden in Folcroft's basement, two floors below.

A press plane had just arrived in Bogotá. It had gone on ahead to record *Air Force One*'s arrival. They would be stalled with a story about weather over the Yucatán Peninsula.

The White House was throwing a lot of attention to the Vice-President's itinerary, obviously hoping by misdirection to keep the domestic press occupied. A major speech by the Vice-President had been announced, one having serious political repercussions.

More misdirection. Unless it too was part of the plot. Smith dismissed that thought. The President's own staff would not throw in with any coup. It made no sense. This was America, not some banana republic. But even as the thought struck Smith, he sat up, realizing that had it not been for CURE, America might be no better than many Latin-American republics struggling against internal disorder.

The ordinary desk phone rang, and Smith reached for it without averting his eyes from the screen.

"Yes?" he said dryly.

"Remo here."

"Progress?"

"We found the Bimbo Bread truck, but it got away."

Smith's hand tightened on the receiver. "The President?"

"He might have been in back, but the V.P. was definitely at the wheel. He drives pretty good too. He got away from us."

"Where are you now?" Smith's voice was bitter.

"In a hotel. The Krystal. That's with a K."

"Return to the field. Every minute counts."

"Wish we could," Remo said worriedly, "but Chiun's incapacitated. I'm not feeling so hot myself."

"What is this?"

"It's the air. The pollution. You know how we function, Smith. Correct breathing, centering. We're weak as kittens."

"I understand nothing of that."

"If you can't breathe, you can't run. Right? If we can't breathe, we can't do the impossible. But we'll manage."

"Remo, I'm getting the CIA warnings out of Mexico of suspected Colombian narco-terrorists converging on Mexico City. What do you know about that?"

"Oh, right. That flashy DFS *comandante* you hooked us up with? We think he's been bought off. It's possible he overheard our last talk."

"Then he knows the President may be alive in Mexico," Smith said in a hoarse tone.

"Afraid so," Remo admitted.

"Therefore these terrorists may be en route to locate or possibly to take possession of the President from whoever's holding him." The long-distance trunkline buzzed over the silence as both men considered the possibility. Finally Smith cleared his throat. His voice was metallic when he spoke again.

"Remo, the President must not fall into the hands of the Colombians."

"Gotcha."

"Remo, it would be better if the President died before he fell into their hands—better for him, and better for America."

"You don't mean—"

"Do you want me to repeat that?" Smith said harshly.

"No, I read you, you cold-blooded son of a bitch," Remo said bitterly.

"Do you remember the story of Enrique Camarena?"

"Should I?"

"He was a DEA agent stationed in Mexico. Corrupt Mexican authorities betrayed him to drug traffickers. They tortured him until they extracted every DEA secret they could. Then they killed him. The President holds many secrets too. Our national security—never mind our nation's prestige—rides on his not falling into the hands of these bloodsuckers."

"I said, I read you," Remo snapped. "Look, we're on it. Is there anyone we can trust down here?"

"No."

"That makes it harder for us. We're handicapped as it is."

"Your best lead will be the local Mexican news," Smith said. "That was the source of the bread-truck tip. Follow any rumor, no matter how bizarre."

"Oh, come on, Smith!" Remo exploded. "We can't hang around watching TV, hoping for a lead."

"You'll do whatever it takes, Remo," Smith said flintily. "But you'll do your job. And stay in constant touch."

"There's another thing," Remo said quickly. "Chiun

thinks the V.P. recognized him. That's why he took off."

"Remo, that's impossible. The President knows what you both look like, but the Vice-President could not."

"You don't suppose the President could have told him about us?" Remo suggested.

Smith's voice was flat. "I cannot believe this President would do any such thing."

"Then can you explain it?"

"No," Smith admitted.

"Well, there it is. Look, we'll stay in touch. You do the same."

"I want results, Remo." Smith hung up on Remo's response. He had work to do.

Down in Mexico City, Remo snapped, "And you'll get them," into the dead phone. He hung up, adding, "You just might not like them. But then, you never do, do you?"

Outside, a violent electrical storm had broken out. Rain came down in sheets of metallic needles. It washed the windows like an invisible car wash. Forked lightning stirred the storm.

Remo turned to Chiun, lying on the bed. "We got to move fast," he said. "Can you hold up your end?"

The Master of Sinanju opened his tired eyes.

"Yes. The rain will cleanse the air of impurities."

"It won't add any oxygen. We're way above sea level."

Chiun slipped his legs over the side of the bed.

"We must do what we can. Where do we begin?"

"Believe it or not," Remo said, picking up the remote-control unit and pointing it at the television set, "we start with the local news. I'll watch. You translate."

He fell back onto the bed, felt something hard dig into his back, and pulled out the videotape of the President's rescue. He tossed it on the nightstand and waited for the TV screen to come to life.

16

The White House staff called it "grips and grins."

After four straight hours of it, the Vice-President of the United States called it agony.

He collapsed in his suite at a local hotel.

"Boy, am I glad that's over!" he told his chief of staff. "I could use a round of golf," he added, squeezing his right hand, "but I think if I get a club in my hand, I won't be able to let go."

"I got bad news for you, Dan."

The Vice-President looked up.

The look on his chief of staff's face was grave. He was pale. His voice had quavered toward the end.

For an instant the universe reeled under the Vice-President of the United States. For an instant he thought the thing he half-hoped and half-dreaded had come to pass. The thing that the nation talked about, joked about, and even feared, each according to his views and political opinions.

"You mean . . . ?" The Vice-President croaked.

"Yes," the chief of staff said. "The White House wants us to go to Detroit and do another one of these damn things."

The Vice-President let out his breath. His heart started beating again. He was not the new President.

"What?" he said dazedly.

"More grips and grins," the chief of staff said grimly. "The White House wants it coordinated with the Bogotá thing."

"Oh," said the Vice-President. He was relieved. He hadn't wanted to become President under these circumstances. But the possibility had been on everyone's lips ever since the President had agreed to go to Colombia.

"I don't know if I can deal with this," the Vice-President admitted, trying to unclench his right hand.

"It's a two-hour flight. Take a nap and soak your hand-shaking hand on the plane. But let's go. They're really anxious about this."

The Vice-President got up and straightened his tie with stiff fingers.

"Oh, by the way," his chief of staff said, pulling out an envelope, "this is for you."

The Vice-President reached for the proffered envelope, but his fingers refused to close around it. It dropped to the carpet.

"I'll get it," said his chief of staff.

"No, I will," the Vice-President said genially.

They bumped heads attempting to retrieve the fallen envelope.

"Sorry."

"No, I'm sorry," the Vice-President said, holding his head.

His chief of staff helped the Vice-President to his feet and again handed him the envelope. This time the Vice-President accepted it with his left hand. The transfer was completed without further incident, much to his chief of staff's surprise. He had known the Vice-President to forget his own wife's name.

The Vice-President looked at the blank white front and asked, "What is it?"

"From the White House. It's your speech."

"My speech?"

"Yeah. They had the President's top speech writer draft it. I think it's tied to the one the President is giving in Bogotá."

"Really?" the Vice-President said, pleased that he rated a presidential speech writer. He reached for the flap.

"No, don't open it now!"

The Vice-President's smile turned to a frown. "Why not?"

"It's not to be opened until you give it."

"How am I gonna practice it?"

"You can't. The White House gave strict orders that you not read it beforehand. There's a covering letter inside explaining that."

"Okay," the Vice-President said, digging at the flap.

"No! You're not supposed to read that until five minutes before the speech."

"This is crazy!"

"The White House chief of staff says it's very, very important. It's a major speech. He says it may be one of the most important of your career."

"This is weird."

"This is politics. And you know how the President is about leaks. Now, come on. We're got a plane to catch."

17

Emilio Mordida wore the stony copper face of a *mestizo*. His expression seldom wavered. It might have belonged on a Mayan rain god. Emilio was of Mayan descent. Also Zapotec, Chichimec, and of course Spanish.

Like most *mestizos*, he had no concept of time. Not even years of working as a desk clerk in the Japanese-owned Nikko Hotel in Mexico City's Zona Hotelera had inculcated him with a shred of punctuality. A wake-up call for seven sharp might be made at seven-fifteen or even seven-fifty-nine. It did not matter. This was Mexico, where the only god was *mañana*.

It was another desultory afternoon in the massive neo-Aztec lobby of the Nikko. Emilio shifted between the computer terminal and the guests checking in and out, looking very modern in his powder-blue jacket, but wearing the immutable mask of his Mexican forebears, one that betrayed no hint of ego or inferiority. It was the mask many Mexicans wore in a land that did not belong to them anymore.

Nothing, not the drumming of impatient fingers on the marble countertop, nor the half-muttered insults by foreign *turistas* who thought they too were the lords of Mexico, brought a flicker of reaction as Emilio went about his methodical unhurried day.

The drone of the fountains was his clock. Unlike the Japanese or the Americans, who saw time as a straight line, Emilio saw time as a bubble—a warm amniotic bubble in which a man might float through life. And so patrons waited while Emilio went on his silent, officious way, his face impassive.

Until a man who bore a strong resemblance to the Vice-President of the United States of America entered the spacious lobby.

Emilio Mordida noticed him because he entered carrying a dusty golf bag. Golf was not unknown in Mexico City, but it hardly rivaled soccer or bullfighting.

Emilio studiously ignored a West German couple who were attempting to check out in time to meet their plane and followed the man with the golf bag with his dark eyes.

Yes, those were definitely golf clubs in the bag. And it was certainly the Vice-President. He walked mechanically, looking neither left nor right, his face a mask as stiff as Emilio's own. Only instead of a sullen set to his mouth, the Vice-President wore a smile that might have been carved of ivory and rose marble.

The Vice-President spurned the reception desk and went directly to the elevators.

It was enough to cause one of Emilio Mordida's inflexible eyelids to lift in surprise.

All morning the city had been buzzing with rumors that the American Vice-President had been seen driving around the city. At first it was said he had been driving a bread truck. Then he was seen at a discotheque dancing with Charro. Or that he had lost two fingers fighting over a bullfighter's woman in the affluent Colonia del Valle district, but had emerged victorious.

Emilio had absorbed these rumors with interest, dismissing them as hysteria in the wake of the imminent arrival of the President in Bogotá. Many had thought that Mexico City was a better—and safer—location for the drug summit. The President of Mexico himself had prevailed on the U.S. President to consider reconvening in Mexico City, but was politely rebuffed.

But here was the Vice-President, clearly the Vice-President. Although it could have been Robert Redford. They looked very much alike.

Emilio, showing uncharacteristic swiftness, fairly leapt to the reservations terminal and punched up the Vice-President's name.

He was not registered, which did not surprise Emilio one bit. Robert Redford was also not listed.

Moving swiftly, Emilio Mordida left the reservations desk and made for the elevator bank.

He was not surprised to see that the Vice-President was still awaiting an elevator. Even the elevators were slow in Mexico.

When one arrived, Emilio followed the Vice-President into the car. The Vice-President pressed sixteen. Emilio then pressed seventeen.

They rode in silence, Emilio watching the Vice-President's boyish, almost ghoulishly smiling profile. He was even younger-looking than he had appeared on television.

The car stopped at the sixteenth floor. The Vice-President stepped off. The doors rolled shut.

Emilio rode to the next floor and slipped back down the stairs.

The Vice-President was still in the corridor, Emilio discovered when he peered around the elevator alcove. He was behaving very strangely. He was going from door to door, putting his ear to each panel. He would listen for a brief instant, then move on.

Until he reached Room 1644. There he paused a bit longer. The Vice-President dropped to his knees with a quick folding of his knee joints and put his eyes to the electronic lock, much as a submarine captain looks through a periscope.

The Nikko's locks required no key, but a magnetized passcard. The lock combinations were changed daily. They could not be breached without the correct card.

Yet, as Emilio watched, the Vice-President proceeded to breach the lock. He accomplished this in a novel, perhaps unique manner. Withdrawing his eyes from the card slot, he lifted his right hand and, retracting his thumb, jammed the remaining four into the slot.

This was an impossibility, Emilio knew. Human fingers are too large for the card-reader slot. But not only did the slot accept them right up to the knuckles, the metal gave no squeal of protest.

Most mysteriously, the red light over the slot turned green, signifying the magnetic card reader recognized the Vice-President's four fingers.

The Vice-President withdrew his remarkable fingers and slipped into the open door. The green light winked out and the red light winked back on. The corridor was silent.

Eyes puzzled, Emilio Mordida passed down the corridor to the door to Room 1644. The lock was as it should be. Undamaged. There was not so much as a scratch around the slot.

Taking a deep breath, he knocked on the door.

After a moment a voice demanded, "Who is there?"

"Hotel staff, *señor*. Is everything satisfactory?"

"Yes. Go away."

"*Sí, señor.*"

Emilio Mordida withdrew to the elevator alcove and looked back around the corner. He saw the door suddenly open, and a multilingual "Do Not Disturb" sign was surreptitiously hung on the doorknob. The door clicked shut again.

All the way down to the lobby, Emilio Mordida thought quickly. This was worth money, this information. The news agencies like Notimex would pay many pesos for such a tip. As would, he supposed, the local police and the Federales.

Returning to his counter, where one of his fellow clerks was stolidly enduring the fractured-Spanish abuse of the West German couple Emilio had earlier ignored, he wondered who would pay the most handsomely for such a tip. The Security Police. Perhaps the Federales.

Emilio checked the reservations terminal, punching up Room 1644. It showed vacant. It had been vacant two days.

As Emilio Mordida dialed the local office of the Federales, he wondered what would compell the Vice-President of the United States to become a squatter in this hotel. Did they not pay him enough?

The Primer Comandante of the Distrito Federal of the FJP haggled with Emilio Mordida only a few moments before proper remuneration was agreed upon. Swiftly Mordida told the *comandante* of the Vice-President's unorthodox residence at the Nikko.

"Who else knows of this?" the *comandante* inquired suspiciously.

"No one, *comandante*."

"See that no one else learns," barked the *comandante*, who abruptly hung up.

Emilio Mordida hung up, confident that within a week—no more than three—a fat envelope would be presented to him by a Federal. Corruption was a way of life in Mexico, but everyone valued a good source. The *comandante* would be true to his word.

Still, Emilio thought, there was always the chance that the *comandante* would forget or his messenger would pocket the money for himself.

Emilio picked up the receiver and began to dial the DFS. He could have saved himself the trouble. For the Federal *comandante* had already sold the DFS the intelligence for three times what had been promised Emilio Mordida.

And so, word was eventually relayed to Tampico Zone Comandante Oscar Odio, who had agreed to remunerate his FJP informant handsomely.

Odio quickly put in a call to Bogotá.

"Padrino," he said.

"*Sí?*"

"I have news, both good and bad."

"I am listening."

"I regret to inform you that your *pistoleros*—I assume it was they—were all annihilated earlier to-day. Their dead bodies were found by my agents beside the Áquila Azteca train, which they attempted to board."

"*Muy triste*," El Padrino hissed, sounding more hateful than sad. In a softer voice he added, "And their quarry?"

"That is the good news I have for you, Padrino. I have been reliably informed that the Vice-President has been located in one of our best hotels."

Odio could hear El Padrino sit up.

"And *el presidente, el jefe,* himself?"

"I do not have that information as yet, but I am working on this."

"Who else knows of this, Odio?"

"By this time," Oscar Odio said truthfully, "probably half the Mexican security appartus."

"I have other assets in the area," El Padrino said smoothly. "But it will take time to move them into position. What can you do to further my interests?"

"The Vice-President is occupying a room illegally," Odio explained. "He can be detained on these grounds."

"Do this, and I promise you, Comandante, you will never stoop to accepting fat envelopes again. You will be passing them out."

"As you say, Padrino."

Comandante Oscar Odio hung up the phone, his wide smile threatening to pierce his earlobes. He put on his mirrored sunglasses and wrapped a silk scarf around his neck.

Outside, the helicopter was waiting. He anticipated trading it in for a newer model by month's end. Perhaps one with rocket pods. Yes, he would enjoy waving rocket pods.

18

Federal Judicial Police Officer Guadalupe Mazatl was forced to give up her search for the *loco* American diplomats. They had disappeared in the controlled confusion of Mexico City traffic more quickly than she would have believed possible. Even the sick Asian one, who looked as if he could barely walk, never mind run.

Officer Mazatl had given up the foot chase and returned to the taxi. After thirty or forty minutes of aimless circling of the Zona Rosa and questioning numerous local police, she decided they were unfindable. There had been no sign of the Bimbo Bread truck, which had compelled them, for some strange reason, to leap into traffic, risking their very lives.

Something strange was happening, Officer Mazatl considered as the taxi drove her to Mexico City FJP headquarters, a white colonial building with the words "POLICIA JUDICIAL FEDERAL DE ESTADO" in gold lettering over the entrance.

The Mexico City *primer comandante* was only too happy to assist Officer Mazatl in her plight.

"You have lost your charge, eh, *chica?*" he said, coming around from his desk. He shut the door. His

162

arm went around Officer Mazatl's shoulders. Officer Mazatl undid the flap of her belt holster. It made a loud snap. The arm withdrew with alacrity.

"You misjudge me, *chica*. You are out of your district. I only wish to assist you."

"They are an Anglo and an old Asian man," Officer Mazatl clipped out. "The Anglo dresses in a black T-shirt. The Oriental wears a fine red silk robe."

"Ah," said the *comandante*. "Yes. I have heard of them."

"They are supposed to be attached to the U.S. embassy."

"If that is so, why have they taken up residence in a hotel?"

"Which hotel?"

"Ah, but if I tell you that, what will you do for me?" His voice was like cream.

"We are *compañeros* of the FJP," Officer Mazatl said tightly. "We should be working together."

The *comandante* smiled generously. "I am, like you, poorly paid, and forced to seek opportunities in order to make my poor way in the world."

"You do not expect me to bribe a fellow officer into sharing police intelligence!" Officer Mazatl flared.

"No, I do not expect it, but . . ." His hands spread like separating birds, lazily taking wing.

"Never mind! I will do my duty without you."

As Officer Mazatl stormed out, the *comandante*'s voice called coolly after her, "When you change your mind, *chica*, I will be here, thinking of your strong womanly body."

It cost Officer Mazatl only ninety pesos and a look at her credentials to commandeer an FJP car from the motor pool. The *comandante* had been too eager to have his way with her. He had admitted the

americano and his friend were registered in a hotel.
There were many, many hotels in Mexico City, it
was true. But it would be infinitely easier to check
with every one of them than to have to bed that
criadero de sapos of a *comandante*.

As she pulled into traffic, Officer Guadalupe Mazatl
noticed the heavy police patrols. On one corner,
three officers stood around talking to one another,
two holding machine guns at the ready, the third
casually swinging a double-barreled shotgun. They
looked tense, even for Mexico City police.

Everywhere there were police. DFS vehicles and
Mexican Army soldiers in their forest-green uni-
forms, all armed, all alert.

Could the downing of *Air Force One* have anything to do with this? Officer Mazatl wondered.

She drove directly for the Zona Rosa, the opulent
and overpriced tourist district. It was near the U.S.
embassy and therefore exactly the place the *gringos*
would go—if they knew where to go in Mexico.

She checked at the desks in the Galería Plaza and
the Calinda Geneve hotels. The *gringos* had not
been there.

Driving down Liverpool, past still-shattered fa-
cades of buildings damaged during the 1985 earthquake, she stopped at the Krystal.

"*Señor, por favor.*" She accosted the desk clerk,
quickly describing Remo and Chiun.

The clerk wordlessly passed her a key. It was
stamped Room 67.

"*Gracias,*" Officer Mazatl said, striding for the
elevator.

She boarded the car with a pair of white-uniformed
waiters carrying covered trays. They joked among
themselves as the car ascended.

"*Sí*," the first one said, "driving a bread truck. Everyone is talking about it."

"I did not know that Bimbo Bread paid so well as to entice an American politician to drive one of their trucks," the other laughed.

"What is this?" Officer Mazatl said suddenly, erasing the smiles from their dark faces with her authoritative tone.

"*Señorita*, we only—"

"Officer," she corrected.

"Officer, I was merely repeating the stories going around that a man very much resembling the Vice-President of the United States was seen in the city driving a Bimbo Bread truck. It is one of those rumors one hears."

"Bimbo Bread. You are certain of this?"

"*Sí*. But it is a joke."

The elevator dinged, and the doors opened onto the sixth floor.

"We shall see who ends up laughing," she said, leaving them to exchange glances and uplifted eyebrows.

At the door to Room 67, Officer Mazatl used the butt of her gun to knock. She struck the panel so hard it shivered. Then she flipped the pistol around until the muzzle was pointed directly at whoever would answer.

The door flew open. It was Remo. Surprisingly, he was unfazed by the sight of her pistol.

"Who is it?" the squeaky voice of Chiun called from behind Remo.

"It's Lupe," Remo called back. "Told you I recognized her knock."

"Send her away."

"I have a pistol," Lupe warned.

"Down here, everyone has a pistol," Remo muttered. "Come in, as long as you're here."

Lupe shut the door behind her. The TV set was on, tuned to an English broadcast on CNN. The old one called Chiun lay on one bed, looking wan. Remo threw himself onto a chair and focused on the TV.

"How are you, old one?" Lupe asked Chiun.

Nodding to the pistol in her hand, Chiun warned, "If you discharge that thing in here, I will kill you."

Lupe almost laughed, but it was not a time for laughter.

"Why did you chase that bread truck?" Lupe demanded of Remo.

"What truck?" Remo asked, filling a water glass with Tehuacán brand mineral water.

"The Bimbo Bread truck with the Vice-President driving it," she said quickly.

Remo stopped pouring. He looked up. He looked to the one called Chiun. The old one looked back.

They shrugged in unison like two puppets attached to the same strings.

Remo spoke first. "Tell us what you know about the Vice-President," he said.

"Only that he is supposed to be in Mexico City."

"How do you know this?" Chiun demanded coldly.

"Everyone in Mexico City is talking of this."

"They are!" Remo said.

"But they think it is a joke. You do not think it is a joke, do you?"

"Look, can we level with you?" Remo asked.

"Remo," Chiun warned, "we are in a strange land. We can trust no one."

"*Silencio, papacito!*" Lupe hissed. Chiun's face wrinkled as if stung. "Go ahead, Señor Yones."

"Call me Remo," Remo said. "Look, I'm kinda

glad you're here. We've been watching TV, hoping to get some news on the situation."

"What situation?"

"You know about *Air Force One* going down."

"I saw the wreck, same as you."

"Well, what you don't know is that the President was carried out of the wreckage alive. Never mind by whom. The important thing is that the Vice-President, or someone who looks exactly like him, rescued him."

"Are you saying that your President is in this city as well?"

"We think so," Remo admitted. "We hope so. And we're trying to find him. We thought we had him, but the truck got away from us."

"No wonder. You were on foot. You should have stayed with me in the car."

"Spilt milk," Remo said.

"*Qué?*"

"It's an expression," Remo said.

"Do not believe him," Chiun interposed. "He sings the same song to me."

"Why do you not check with your embassy people?" Lupe demanded. "Would your President not seek refuge there?"

"That's the tricky part," Remo explained. "We're not sure the Vice-President is up to any good. This could all be part of a plot."

"It *is* a plot," Chiun intoned feebly from the bed. "The President of Vice's plot."

Lupe frowned. "These things do not happen in American politics," she suggested.

"That's what we thought," Remo sighed. He took a sip of water.

"They happen in all politics," Chiun said firmly.

"So what do you say?" Remo asked Lupe. "Give us a hand?"

"You are in my charge. We will work together as long as you understand that Mexican jurisdiction applies." She pronounced it "yurisdiction."

"Anything you say. Are you ready, Little Father?"

"He is too ill to accompany us," Lupe said firmly.

The old Oriental's eyes narrowed to slits at that remark. He pressed his thin-fingered hands with their impossibly long nails into the bedclothes as if testing the mattress strength.

Without warning, he was suddenly in the air. He executed a smart back flip, landing behind Lupe. She whirled, her gun still in hand.

By the time she turned all the way around, the old one was no longer there and her gun had left her fingers.

She was aware only of her suddenly stinging fingers and a simultaneous flash of crimson silk.

She turned again, and the old Asian was standing there offering her gun back.

Officer Guadalupe Mazatl accepted the pistol in stunned silence. It felt lighter than it should. She broke open the cylinder and saw the chambers were vacant.

"Where are my bullets?" Officer Mazatl sputtered.

"Perhaps you left them in your other gun?" the one called Chiun sniffed.

"I have them," Remo said as he stood up.

He showed her his fist, opening it. Six brass bullets lay in his palm.

"I may need those," she sputtered.

"We don't like wild shooting when we go to work," Remo said, brushing past her for the door, "and we're going to work right now."

Officer Guadalupe Mazatl followed them out into the corridor, trying to reholster her pistol. She was so nervous it took her four tries to get the barrel to go in properly.

Out on the curb, Remo Williams got behind the wheel one step ahead of Lupe Mazatl.

"This is an official vehicle," she snapped. "My vehicle."

"Then you can sit up in front with me," Remo said politely. "That okay with you, Chiun?"

The Master of Sinanju nodded and eased into the back seat. Remo put his hand out the window for the keys.

Officer Mazatl folded her arms angrily.

"Trade you for some bullets?" Remo suggested.

"No."

Remo peered under the dash. "Maybe I can hot-wire it, then."

"Very well," Officer Mazatl said reluctantly.

She got in and they made the exchange.

As Remo started the engine, Offficer Mazatl looked into her open palm. "You gave me only two bullets," she complained.

"I don't remember talking numbers," Remo said, smiling as he pulled into traffic.

"You think you are so smug," Lupe spat.

"Just doing what comes naturally," Remo retorted. "So where do we go first?"

"Yust drive. I will ask questions. First, did either of you see the license plate of the Bimbo Bread truck?"

"Not me," Remo admitted. He called over his shoulder, "You, Chiun?"

"Yes," Chiun said in a tired squeak. "It had some numbers on it. I do not remember what they were."

"Do you remember the letters under the numbers?" Lupe asked.

"Possibly."

"Did they say 'Mex Mex' or 'D.F. Mex'?"

"They said 'D.F. Mex.' I do not know what that could mean."

"It means the truck is registered here in the Distrito Federal, not in the state of Mexico, which surrounds Mexico City."

"That narrows the search area, huh?" Remo suggested.

Lupe picked up a CB-style dashboard microphone. "It would until you understand that Mexico City is the largest city in the world."

"Oh, right. Forgot about that," Remo said.

Lupe began speaking rapid words in Spanish, asking questions and getting answers as Remo tooled his way through the colorful Zona Rosa.

"Take the Paseo de la Reforma," she said suddenly.

"Glad to," Remo shot back. "What is it and where is it?"

She replaced the mike. "Two streets more, then right."

Remo went up a street called Hamburgo and found himself on the same broad avenue where he had earlier lost the bread truck.

"We are passing the American embassy," Lupe said suddenly.

"Is that so?" Remo said, glancing at the flag-draped building.

"Did you not tell me that you worked for the American embassy?" Lupe said harshly.

Remo's face assumed a guileless expression. "We do. Sort of. We're cultural attachés."

"That means CIA."

"No flies on you," Remo said.

"*Qué?*"

"Another expression. The rough translation is, yes, I do work for the CIA. I even have some ID on me. Satisfied?"

"No.

"So where to now?" Remo asked casually.

"Follow Reforma," Lupe said. "I am told a Bimbo Bread truck has been found parked near the Zona Hotelera. It has been abandoned."

"Damn," Remo said softly. He pressed the accelerator to the floor. "That's our only lead."

They skirted Chapultepec Park on one side and the Museum of Anthropology with its battered stone idol on the other, and whizzed past several more humanistic statues Remo didn't recognize.

"The truck will be found on the left, past this next crossroad," Lupe said, pointing.

"We call them intersections," Remo said, slowing down.

Beyond Chapultepec Park, in the shadow of the Hotel Nikko, was a shopping center. They found the truck there, guarded by two stone-faced local policemen toting shotguns.

Officer Mazatl led Remo and Chiun up to the truck, saying, "These *norteamericanos* are with me."

The cops withdrew under Lupe's hard stare and superior credentials. She threw open the back doors.

Loaves of bread tumbled out, several of them torn open and spilling half-eaten slices of thin-sliced bread.

Remo grabbed one bag as it tumbled out. It was crushed, as if stepped or sat upon.

"Looks like someone was in back, in the dark, having himself a pretty plain meal," Remo suggested.

"The true President," Chiun hissed.

Lupe went around to the driver's seat and threw open the door. She looked under the cushions, felt the floorboards, and came back, her face unhappy.

"There are no traces of anyone," she said, sullen-voiced.

"Assuming this is the right truck," Remo asked her intently, "where could they have gone?"

Lupe looked around. "Into any of these places," she said, gesturing toward the cluster of boutiques, theaters, and nightclubs around them. "Or"—her other arm indicated the other side of the Paseo de la Reforma, which hummed with cars and buses and mini-vans—"perhaps into the hotel district. The best hotels in the city are to be found there."

"I don't suppose you could organize a building-to-building search?" Remo wondered, daunted by the task.

"I do not think so," Lupe added unhappily. "I cannot get the local *comandante* to help us. With these burros we must plow."

"What's that?"

"A—how you say?—expression."

Remo winced. "How about these guys?" he suggested, pointing to the police officers standing out of hearing.

"I will speak with them."

Lupe engaged the two officers in earnest conversation and returned to Remo and Chiun.

"They say they are under orders to guard this truck, and not to interfere," she reported.

"Interfere with what?" Remo demanded.

"They refused to say."

"Is something going on?" Remo wondered.

"Something is always going on in Mexico City. It is a cesspool of intrigues. That is why I work in Tampico. There is less money to be had in Tampico, but also less intrigue. I do not understand what is going on."

"Well, nothing to do but to fan out and look around," Remo said morosely. "It's all we have." He turned to Chiun. "Are you up to this, Little Father?"

"No. But anything to get us out of this land of unbreathable air and unfeminine women."

"What did he say?" Lupe demanded.

"Don't sweat it," Remo returned. "He says that about all women—unless they're Korean."

"He is Korean, then?"

"Can't you tell?" Remo asked, without humor.

They split up and went through the various establishments, finally rendezvousing beside the bread truck an hour later, empty-handed and unhappy.

"Well," Remo said, looking around. "Do we do this in quadrants, zones, or what?"

Officer Lupe Mazatl's answer froze in her mouth.

An olive military helicopter suddenly passed overhead, flying slowly and sweeping around. In the distance came the caterwauling of sirens.

The helicopter descended on a strip of grass near the Hotel Nikko.

"That resembles Comandante Odio's helicopter," Lupe said slowly.

"Just what I was thinking," Remo said. "Let's check it out."

Traffic on the Reforma was so heavy in both directions—it seemed to consist of three mini-vans for every single passenger automobile—that the only safe way to cross was a footbridge constructed of loose planks laid on a framework of orange-painted pipes.

It turned out to be only slightly safer than crossing on a strand of spider silk. The framework hummed and rattled in sympathy with the traffic below. The planking was as loose as the teeth in a centuries-old skull.

Eventually they made it over to the other side.

They rounded a corner past a seemingly unfinished statue of a scowling Winston Churchill and into the back entrance of the Nikko, only five paces behind Comandante Oscar Odio's swaggering figure.

Remo caught Lupe's eye and put his finger in front of his lips. She frowned but went along.

They hung back while Comandante Odio strode up to the reception desk and said loudly in Spanish, "This lobby is under DFS control. No one must be allowed to enter or leave."

"Sí, Comandante," a clerk said meekly.

"Which one of you is Emilio?"

A man in a powder-blue coat lifted a hand. His eyes were frightened.

"In what room does your unauthorized guest reside?" Odio's voice was a silken hiss.

"Sixteen-forty-four, señor."

"Sounds good to me," Remo muttered to Chiun, after the Master of Sinanju translated the exchange. To Lupe he said, "Just follow us."

Remo and Chiun flitted through the lobby, going from sofa to plant, unseen by Comandante Odio. Lupe moved between them, feeling very exposed. She was astonished when they reached the elevators unseen.

Remo stabbed the up button. The doors opened

instantly, taking them all by surprise. They rode the elevator to the sixteenth floor in silence.

When the doors separated, Remo stepped out into the corridor.

"The coast looks clear," he said, waving them on.

"What coast?" Lupe hissed. "This is a hotel."

"Expression," Remo said wearily.

They crept to the door of 1644. Remo noticed Lupe extracting her pistol from its holster.

"Put that thing away before I break it over your head," he said harshly. "I don't want any wild shooting if the President's around."

"But it is the only weapon we have among us," Lupe snapped back.

At that, the Master of Sinanju lifted a single gleaming fingernail to Lupe's nose. It hovered there an instant, so close to her face that Lupe's eyes crossed. Then it sliced down with guillotine swiftness.

The leading half-inch of Lupe Mazatl's pistol snapped off, along with the gun sight. Chiun caught it. He presented her with the snapped-off section of the gun barrel in silence.

Officer Mazatl spent a disbelieving second putting the two sections together. They fitted perfectly, but did not adhere.

Swallowing several times, she returned her pistol to its holster.

"*Comprendo?*" Remo asked.

"The proper word," Lupe said hoarsely, "is *comprende.*"

"All my Spanish comes from *Cisco Kid* reruns," Remo said. "Now, get set. We're going in."

Chiun set himself on one side of the door. At a gesture from Remo, Lupe stationed herself on the other.

"You will go in last, old one," she told Chiun.

The Master of Sinanju snorted derisively. "Each monkey to his rope," he said. Lupe frowned at the familiar saying.

Remo pressed the heel of his hand to the electronic-lock assembly. He drew his elbow back and then rammed forward.

The sound that the fracturing assembly made was not loud. But the door itself shot off its hinges like a cannon ball.

Lupe plunged in instantly. To her astonishment, she was still several paces behind Remo and the old Korean. They stopped suddenly, blocking her view.

"Hold it right there!" Remo shouted.

"Make no rash moves, traitor!" Chiun cried.

"What is happening?" Lupe demanded, unable to see past their backs in the narrow foyer.

The bed creaked. Then there was a whisk of a sound, like a sword coming out of its scabbard. Lupe reflexively reached for her pistol again.

Then the fight began. Something flashed past Remo's shoulder. He ducked under the blur and Chiun moved in, kicking high.

A man dropped faster than seemed humanly possible under Chiun's leaping crimson figure. There came another flash of steel, like a sword blade in motion. A cry.

And something shot past Lupe's head with the velocity of a rocket-propelled grenade. She turned around. Embedded in the bathroom door was the laminated maple head of a driver.

Lupe whirled back, and beheld the stunning sight of the Vice-President of the United States lifting a

headless golf club to defend himself as Remo and
Chiun closed in from opposite sides.

"Watch it, Chiun," Remo warned. "He's faster
than you'd think with that thing."

"It is only because we are slowed by this infernal
bad air."

"Just watch it."

The Vice-President looked at his maimed club.
Without a flicker of his fixed expression, he tossed it
aside and extracted a sand wedge. He faced them
boldly, his grin like a photograph.

"If you think you can hurt us with a sand wedge,
you're crazy," Remo said. "Now, put that down and
we'll talk. It's not too late to straighten this out."

"Isn't it?" the voice of the Vice-President said as
he took the steel sand-wedge head in one hand. He
exerted momentary pressure. The metal went *grunk!*
loudly, and when he let go, the head had a sudden
sharp edge.

Remo blinked. "Where'd you learn to do that?" he
demanded, dumbfounded.

The edge sliced for Remo's face. He faded back,
lifting his right hand to parry the next blow, while
Chiun slipped around behind their assailant.

"No good, pal," Remo said. "But go ahead. Take
your Mulligan."

The club came back for another blow. Good, Remo
thought. He's falling for it.

Then the crinkled blue eyes shifted right.

The figure of the Vice-President shifted like a spun
top. Remo couldn't believe his speed. Or was it that
his own senses and reflexes were so slowed by pollution inhalation? he wondered.

The gleaming edge snapped around. It went *whisk!*

whack! furiously, narrowly missing Chiun on both swings.

"Be careful, Little Father," Remo hissed. "He's really, really fast."

"No one is faster than a Master of Sinanju," Chiun cried, and his nails began weaving a defensive pattern before him until their reflection became a silver-shard pattern of light.

The club descended. It bounced off the whirling barrier. The Vice-President lifted it again, this time with both hands.

That gave Remo his opportunity. He plunged in, his hands reaching for the Vice-President's smoothly tonsured neck.

The sand wedge broke off on the second blow. Remo's fingertips brushed the Vice-President's neck hairs for a brief instant.

And then, so quickly that he couldn't believe it, he was holding empty air, and his momentum was carrying him directly into the path of Chiun's deadly flashing nails!

19

DFS Comandante Oscar Odio waited impatiently in the Hotel Nikko lobby for his blue-uniformed agents to arrive. Their sirens filled the air, but they had not yet arrived. He had contacted them as soon as he reached Mexico City airspace, obtaining instant use of a contingent of agents—no questions asked—from the Distrito Federal *comandante*, with whom Odio had a working relationship. It was that simple.

The unit burst into the lobby from all doors like busy blue locusts.

Comandante Odio gave quick orders, stationing men at every exit.

"The remainder of you will follow me!" he cried, brandishing his pistol. *"Vamos!"*

They surged up the stairs because it seemed like the most macho thing to do, even though it was a sixteen-floor climb.

By the time they reached their floor, they were perspiring and out of breath. Even men accustomed to the city's rarefied air suffered it effects.

Officer Guadalupe Mazatl stood blinking at the impossibility of it all.

She saw three *gringos*, Remo and Chiun and apparently the American Vice-President, fighting like demons with fire in their veins and steel in their bones. Their hands moved like quicksilver.

It was not a battle of men, but of gods, much like the old gods of old Mexico to whom Officer Lupe Mazatl had prayed to as a child in the Catholic church whose altar displayed the Virgin of Guadalupe, after whom she was named, but behind which were hidden the true gods of Mexico, Quetzalcoatl, Tezcatlipoca, and Coatlicue.

They were swifter than the hummingbird, more ferocious than the ocelot. Even the Vice-President, with his ridiculous weapons. Lupe could hear the air crack as his club tore through it. He was beating in all directions at once, like some out-of-control machine.

As she watched, the conflict moved swiftly from attack to joined battle to resolution.

No sooner had the deadly sand wedge broken off against a spiderweb of light woven by the one called Chiun than Remo moved in to take the Vice-President by the back of the neck.

Lupe blinked. It seemed as if Remo had the man for certain. And in that blink, the Vice-President was suddenly gone, as if he had turned invisible.

And Remo, unable to check his lunge, was falling into that deadly web of light.

So many things happened in that next breathless instant that Lupe was never sure in what order they transpired.

The shouting at the door behind her first drew her attention. But the crash of shattering glass pulled her head back around again. She blinked rapidly, unable to comprehend what was happening.

"What is going on here?" a familiar voice shouted arrogantly.

Lupe was yanked to her feet and shoved aside by a in-rushing tide of men.

"You!" the voice blurted.

"And you," Lupe said, recognizing Comandante Odio.

"What is going on here!" Odio demanded.

"It's the Vice-President," Remo shouted, his voice twisting like metal in a forge. "He committed suicide!"

"What!" Odio said, racing past Lupe. His DFS forces followed him. Two hung back, seizing Lupe.

"Look!" Remo said, pointing out the big picture window, whose frame was festooned with dangling glass teeth.

Odio rushed to the pane. He looked down.

"*Madre!*" he shouted hoarsely. "It is true!"

Far below, sprawled on the circular driveway facing the Paseo de la Reforma, lay a tiny human figure, a golf bag across his back, spilling various woods and irons.

Odio turned to Remo. "It is the Vice-President?" he demanded.

"He jumped," Remo repeated, sick of voice. "What made him jump?"

"What I would like to know is, what made him so strong?" Chiun put in. He leaned out the window. His nose wrinkled at the sting of foul air in his delicate nostrils. Just as quickly, he withdrew.

"You are all under arrest!" Comandante Odio said swiftly.

"On what charge?" Remo wanted to know.

"The murder of your own Vice-President, *asasino!*"

"It was self-defense," the Master of Sinanju said haughtily. "I challenge you to prove differently."

"I will not have to," Odio retorted. "Here in my country, a man is judged guilty until proved innocent. As you will be if I take you into custody."

Remo pulled himself away from the window.

"If?" he asked shortly.

"It is possible an arrangement could be reached," Odio said smoothly.

Officer Lupe Mazatl spoke up. "What did I tell you about this *hombre?* The DFS all drink from the same little jug."

"*Silencio*, woman!" Odio spat. He turned to Remo. "I would trade you your freedom for a certain thing I require."

"How much?" Remo asked in contempt. He reached into his pocket.

"Oh, it is not a matter of money, but intelligence."

"He thinks you are the Wizard of Ooze Remo," Chiun sniffed. "Do not give him your brain, under any circumstance."

"No, no," Odio said. "I desire information. That is all."

Remo pulled his hand from his pocket. "Yeah?"

"The whereabouts of your *presidente*."

"What makes you think I know that?" Remo asked suspiciously.

"I know that he is in Mexico," Odio said with ill-disguised pride.

"So you *were* listening in," Remo said.

"*Si*."

"On my conversation with Smith?" Remo prodded.

"*Si*, with Smith. Your CIA agent contact, no doubt. The DFS has a working relationship with the CIA. Smith is a *muy* popular name at the CIA. I myself have met many CIA Smiths."

"Good guess," Remo said, his eyes narrowing. His glance flicked to the Master of Sinanju. Chiun nodded imperceptibly.

Remo smiled easily. "Okay. I don't want to be

thrown into a Mexican jail. I hear conditions are pretty terrible—unless you're a drug dealer and can afford a bridal suite."

"You are an intelligent *gringo*," Odio said, his tense expression relaxing. "Now I give you my word. Provide me with the information and I will set you free. But you must leave the country immediately.

"Sure thing," Remo said casually. "He's right behind you. In the closet."

Comandante Oscar Odio's eyes went wide with surprise. Eagerly he turned to give the order to search the closet to his borrowed DFS unit.

His mouth opened. His arm raised. The arm froze and his mouth locked, as a stiffened finger stabbed at the nape of his neck, shattering vertebrae like ice cubes. The disintegrating bone severed his spinal cord so swiftly that Comandante Oscar Odio had only time to exhale the first breathy consonant of his order. His brain died before his face hit the rug.

The others failed to see the blow that felled him. They were too busy dying. The Master of Sinanju crushed a convenient kidney with one fist and jellied testicles with a high-kicking sandaled foot.

Remo waded in to help, pitching one DFS agent out the shattered window and lifting another off his feet bodily. He threw that one toward the door, where the remaining DFS agents had Officer Mazatl in custody.

"Duck!" Remo said quickly.

"*Qué?*" they said in unison.

"Too late," Remo said as the flying body bowled Officer Lupe Mazatl and her captors out into the hall.

Remo leapt after them, and quickly crushed the DFS men's windpipes with the heel of one Italian loafer. He gave Officer Mazatl a hand, bringing her to her feet with a smooth retraction of his arm.

"You killed them all," Officer Lupe Mazatl said in a dazed voice.

"And on our worst day, too," Remo said. He plunged back into the room, where the Master of Sinanju was opening the closet. It was empty.

"Too bad," Remo said, looking in. "I had my hopes he'd have been stashed there."

"You killed five DFS officers with your bare hands," Officer Mazatl said, her voice tight and sick.

"They knew too much," Remo said. "Come on. We've got to go to Plan B."

"What is Plan B?" Lupe wanted to know as she was pulled by one hand out the door and to the elevators.

"Be prepared to improvise," Remo said bitterly. "First we check the Vice-President. Maybe he has something on him that'll help."

"Such as?"

"A safe-deposit-box key or a bus-terminal-locker tag," Remo growled unhappily. "I don't know. Look, I just had the Vice-President of the United States attack me and then take a header out an open window. I'm having a terrible day."

"Do not worry," Chiun put it. "I will vouch for you with Smith. None of this would have happened had Smith not sent us after ferocious geese."

"That's going to mean a lot, if we don't locate the President," Remo said sourly.

The elevator brought them to the lobby, where they were greeted by two DFS officers with drawn pistols.

The officers said, *"Alto!"* and Remo returned their greeting by cracking their pelvises with a swift upkick to each man.

He left them writhing on the floor, not exactly dead, but in no mood to celebrate life.

The lobby was free of other human encumbrances. In fact, it was deserted.

"It is not like one such as Odio not to have the lobby guarded by more men than those two," Lupe said as they made for the main entrance.

"I'm not complaining," Remo growled.

Out in the circular driveway, they discovered why the lobby was empty. Everyone was out there—DFS agents and Nikko employees alike—standing in the broken glass and staring at a body.

Remo pushed through the crowds. A DFS officer pushed back. Without looking, Remo casually batted with the back of his hand. The agent's head jumped off his shoulders with a report like a mushy cannon shot and struck a nearby bronze horse.

That got the crowd's attention. They backed off with gape-mouthed respect.

Remo knelt beside the body. It was dressed in a blue DFS uniform. It was the one he had pitched out the window. "Damn!" he breathed.

Jumping to his feet, Remo raced through the crowd. Everywhere he went, a path was cleared for him. A few people panicked and ran off. There were no other bodies.

"I don't see the V.P.!" Remo called to Chiun. "Where is he?"

Officer Lupe Mazatl demanded the same question of the crowd. One of the DFS officers meekly replied, and she translated for Remo's benefit.

"He says there is only one body, that one."

"Well, I saw the Vice-President lying right here," Remo snapped. "He didn't just get up and walk away."

Lupe put the question to the DFS agent.

"He says that they heard a crash of glass," she said, translating the man's voluable Spanish. "They came out and saw nothing but a man with a golf bag walking away."

Remo blinked. "Then what?"

"Then the DFS officer fell from the sky."

Remo looked to Chiun. "Is she translating it right?" he wanted to know.

The Master of Sinanju nodded. "The President of Vice got up and walked away. But it is not possible."

"Not possible?" Remo snorted. "It's ridiculous."

Officer Mazatl put in her two cents. "I have read that it is a great puzzle why your *presidente* picked that man to be his second."

"Yeah?" Remo said slowly.

"A man who can fall sixteen stories and walk away is a man. What we call *mucho hombre*. It is no wonder he was chosen."

Remo blinked some more. "That almost makes sense," he said.

"Enough," Chiun snapped. He turned to the DFS agent and rattled off a string of Spanish questions.

"He says our quarry walked in that direction, toward Chapultepec Park," Chiun translated.

Remo looked across the Paseo de la Reforma, where the thick green of the park shivered in the passing hurricane of traffic.

"Then we start our search there!" Remo said. "Come on!"

No one got in their way as they ran for the side street, Calzada Arquimedes, and to the Reforma.

They stood on the corner of Arquimedes and the Reforma, beside the glowering statue of Winston Churchill, who looked as if he were emerging from a mud slide. Comandante Odio's helicopter sat on a nearby traffic island, its rotors drooped.

The traffic was like a fast-moving wall that spewed noxious fumes in their faces.

Almost immediately, Remo became aware of the tight band encircling his head.

He looked to the Master of Sinanju.

"Oh-oh, I'm starting to feel woozy again," he said.

"I too," said Chiun.

"It is because you have been exerting yourselves," Lupe told them. "You must not run."

"We gotta," Remo said. "Finding the Vice-President is our responsibility. He's our only lead to the President."

"If you faint, then, do not blame me," Lupe said flatly.

"Little Father?" Remo said.

Chiun lifted a wise finger. "We will not run," he announced. "But we will walk very fast."

"Maybe we'd better split up?" Remo suggested.

"Yes. We will take opposite sides of the street," Chiun said. "I will allow you to cross the traffic," he added.

"Thanks," Remo said dryly. "Let's try to maintain eye contact until one of us spots something. It's gonna take both of us to catch the Vice-President— especially in our present condition." Remo turned to Lupe. "Mind staying with him?"

"Of course not, I prefer it," Lupe said tartly.

Remo looked back and saw the orange-pipe foot-bridge. He used it to reach the other side of the Reforma.

Once there, Remo walked along the broad shady sidewalk, keeping pace with Chiun and Guadalupe on the other side.

On his side, Chapultepec Park was bound by an iron fence. As Remo walked, he noticed bushes sculptured into the shapes of animals—a ram, a llama, and a particularly joyful-looking hippopotamus—on the other side of the fence. A little farther on, he spied a miniature railroad through the thick foliage. Probably the children's section of the park, he concluded.

Through the trees beyond, Remo saw no sign of the Vice-President, who by all accounts should be lying in a pool of blood and glass back in front of the hotel.

He couldn't figure it out. What was the deal here? Like many Americans, Remo had been mystified by the selection of an obscure Hoosier senator to be elevated to the vice-presidency. There was obviously more to the man than anyone had thought, if today's events meant anything.

Maybe that was it, Remo thought. Maybe he was the President's secret weapon. This President had once considered shutting down CURE. But if that was the case, why, after rescuing him, had the Vice-President hidden the President?

Across the Reforma, the Master of Sinanju crossed a side street to a brick-paved park dominated by a tall bronze statue of a man in military uniform. Probably some Mexican general, Remo thought. He walked on.

He came to a huge wrought-iron gate. It was closed. Remo looked back to the other side of the Reforma, saw the Master of Sinanju stopped before the bronze statue, head cocked inquisitively, and waved. Chiun did not look in his direction. He seemed fascinated by the statue for some reason. Probably Lupe was explaining its historical importance.

"Great," he muttered. "We're only trying to rescue the President, and those two are playing tourist and native guide."

Remo hesitated. The thrum of traffic was like a wall of sound. No point in trying to yell. He decided to go over the fence, knowing that if the Vice-President had entered the park, every minute counted.

The Master of Sinanju walked slowly, deliberately. His magnificent lungs drew in empowering oxygen. The trouble was, it tasted like nitrogen coming in, and with each exhalation, Chiun felt as if he were venting precious life-giving oxygen.

"This is a dirty place," he said, giving his opinion of Mexico City to the Mexican woman named Guadalupe. "It is no wonder that my ancestors had nothing to do with the Aztecs."

"Were I in your country, I would not criticize it," Guadalupe said sullenly.

"You would not like my country. The air is breathable."

They came to a red-brick park on the corner of Reforma and Calzada Mahatma Gandhi. There stood a more-than-life-size bronze statue of a man, hands clasped behind his back, on a dais. The edge of the dais bore a name: JOSIP BROZ TITO.

Chiun walked past the statue of the unimportant non-Korean and through the park, where stylized grasshoppers perched on stone hieroglyphs.

Something silvery gleamed in the bushes directly behind the bronze statue. The Master of Sinanju abruptly swerved toward that unexpected gleam.

"What are you doing?" Guadalupe asked as the Master of Sinanju bent at the waist and reached into the bushes.

He stood up, frowning at the sand wedge in his hand.

"What?" Lupe gasped.

"The bag and remaining clubs are also here," Chiun said solemnly.

Guadalupe joined him. "He must have cast them aside," she ventured.

Ignoring her, Chiun looked around the park.

"His clothes are also here," Guadalupe said. "Why would he discard his clothes?" she asked in puzzlement, holding up a brown jacket by its collar.

The Master of Sinanju did not reply. He had found the shoes and socks that had been discarded behind a tree. Shoes did not always leave imprints, but bare feet did—even on brick, the outline of perspiration could be seen by eyes that had been sharpened by Sinanju training.

The Master of Sinanju did not find any perspiration imprints when he examined the brick sidewalk, however. He floated back to the bushes, where the Mexican woman stood, a befuddled expression on her impassive brown face.

There were heavy footprints in the soft dirt, he saw. They led directly to the statue's austere dark bronze back.

His facial wrinkles multiplying in thought, Chiun went around to the front. He looked up. His eyes narrowed. It was merely a statue, its eyes lifted skyward.

Chiun looked down. Flecks of dirt collected at the statue's booted feet. No crumbs of soil lay outside the circumference of the dais, however. And no perspiration imprints were visible on it.

Guadalupe joined him, regarding the statue. They stood in silence for many moments, Chiun's hands withdrawing into his sleeves, which joined over his stomach.

Finally the Master of Sinanju put a question to her.

"How long has this statue been at this spot?" he asked softly, not taking his eyes off its metallic face.

"I do not know," Lupe admitted. "I am in Mexico City only from time to time. Why?"

"Have you seen it here before?"

"Sí. It has been here several years, in recognition of the close ties between my government and this man, who formerly headed Yugoslavia."

Chiun stepped up to the dais. One fingernail lifted cautiously. He tapped the bronze once. It rang faintly—a solidly metallic ring. The true and correct ring of bronze.

"What do you do?" Guadalupe asked slowly.

"Hush," Chiun admonished. He brushed a cloud of hair away from one delicate ear and placed it to the statue's stomach, the highest point he could monitor without lifting up on tiptoe.

Guadalupe watched him with growing concern. She had heard of tourists fainting in the thin air, who had to be hospitalized during the winter months, when the natural bowl that was Mexico City trapped inversions along with the terrible pollution.

But she had never before heard of a *gringo* who had become crazed by the bad air. And this old one was not even, strictly speaking, a *gringo*.

As she watched, the Master of Sinanju's brow crinkled. His parchment face gathered like drying papier-mâché. His tiny mouth popped open suddenly.

He stepped back abruptly. "I hear sounds," he whispered in a surprised voice.

"What kind of sounds?"

"Metal sounds."

"It is made of *bronce*," Lupe said reasonably. "Of course you would hear metal sounds."

"Not like these," Chiun said, regarding the statue with suspicious eyes. "These are clicks and hums, the sounds of gears and other machine workings."

"But it is a statue. It is hollow."

"It is not hollow, although it may be a statue."

At the sound of those words, the statue, whose head had been tilted slightly upward toward the brownish sky, suddenly looked down. Its bronze neck creaked with the impossible movement.

"*Dios!*" Guadalupe gasped. She stepped back without thinking, her hand reaching for her pistol.

The eyes of the statue, with its hollow shadowed pupils, moved, showing a sudden dark gleam, like obsidian lenses. And the sculptured mouth dropped open.

The statue spoke, evoking a shriek from Guadalupe Mazatl.

"*Why do you pursue me?*" Josip Broz Tito asked, his voice a conglomeration of raspy metallic vowels and consonants, like dozens of hasps and files sawing one another, trying to make articulate music.

"It speaks!" Lupe gasped. "The statue is speaking!"

"Because you are the Vice-President, statue," the Master of Sinanju said in a reasonable tone. He did not understand what would possess a statue to talk, but he knew that when faced with the unknown, a wise assassin did not show fear. He repressed it.

"*I am not the Vice-President now,*" the statue of Josip Broz Tito said through gnashing teeth.

"True," returned the Master of Sinanju carefully. His eyes narrowed. There was something familiar about the way this statue spoke. Not the tortured metallic voice, but the too-simple manner of phrasing. He pressed on.

"There is another reason I pursue you," Chiun added firmly.

"I would like to know that reason."

"Why?"

"It is important to me."

"Why is it important to you, O statue?" the Master of Sinanju asked carefully.

"It is important to my survival."

"Ahhh," said the Master of Sinanju, and he knew what the statue truly was.

But knowing the truth and admitting it were different matters. The Master of Sinanju preferred not to let the statue know that he knew what he knew.

"It is important to me to know that the President is safe," Chiun said simply.

"He is safe," the statue said.

"How do I know this?"

"Because I am not lying," said the statue with invincible logic.

"I see," mused the Master of Sinanju. "It is also important that I see this for myself. It is my responsibility to see that the President is returned to his own country in safety. He has many enemies in this land."

"This is important to me as well, meat machine."

The Master of Sinanju let the odd description pass. It only confirmed what he already knew.

"Perhaps we can assist each other in our mutual goal, O strange statue."

"Explain."

"Take me to the President, and I will conduct him to his home. He will be safe with me, and you will be relieved of your burden."

"No."

"Why not?"

"I must accompany the President wherever he goes."

"Why is this necessary if I give you my word that he will be safe?"

"Because I do not trust your word. And I must be with the President at all times."

"Why?"

"I am safe with him. He is well-protected. The meat machines work very hard to ensure his survival. All persons and machines around him are ensured of their survival. My survival will therefore be assured so long as we are inseparable."

"Well-spoken," said Chiun. "But you are not with him now."

"This is a temporary necessity," Josip Broz Tito grated. *"Evil meat machines are attempting to terminate him. Until I have devised a safe method to return him to his habitation, I have placed him in a secure place.*

"Where, O statue?"

"I will not tell you. You may mean harm to him. I cannot allow that, for it threatens my survival."

"I understand perfectly, O mysterious statue whose true nature is unknown to me," Chiun said broadly. "Perhaps I can help you in your plight."

"Explain."

"What are you doing?" Lupe demanded. "You cannot bargain with a statue. It does not live."

"I will offer you safe passage back to America," Chiun went on, ignoring the outburst, "you and the true President, where you will be safe."

The statue hesitated. Its mouth stood open, but no grinding words issued forth.

"More information," it said at last.

"I work for the President's government," the Master of Sinanju said proudly. "I cannot tell you how, for it is a secret. But I will report to my emperor, and tender to him any offer you wish to make. I am certain he will barter your survival for the President's safety."

"This would solve my dilemma," the statue said rackingly.

"If you will remain here, I will make contact with my emperor," said Chiun.

A bronze arm lifted in warning. *"No. I do not trust you. We will meet in another place."*

Chiun nodded. "Where?"

"I do not know the names of places in this city." The statue's head swiveled like a football on a bronze spit. It groaned horribly.

Guadalupe Mazatl recoiled from the statue's inhuman regard.

"You, indigenous female meat machine. Name a place where there are no others like you in great numbers."

"Teotihuacán," Lupe sputtered. "It is a ruined city. To the north. Very large. Very empty. That would be a place such as you wish."

"In three hours," the statue intoned, *"I will await you in Teotihaucán."*

"Done," said the Master of Sinanju, executing a quick bow.

And then the Master of Sinanju beheld a sight such as he had never before seen in his many decades in the West.

The bronze statue lifted one foot. One bronze boot wrenched free of its base, leaving a shiny irregular patch. The other foot snapped loose.

Then, arms creaking, legs bending to the tortured shriek and snarl of bronze, the statue of Josip Broz Tito walked off its pedestal and marched away, stiff and ungainly as an old stop-motion mechanical man.

It stamped up the Paseo de la Reforma back in the direction of the Hotel Nikko.

"Increible!" Guadalupe said hoarsely. She made a

slow sign of the cross, but the words she muttered were ancient Nauatl, and the gods she invoked were of old Mexico, not the East.

The Master of Sinanju watched as the bronze figure, its head jerking right, then left, then right again as it walked, went to the waiting helicopter and climbed aboard.

The rotors started turning. The engines whined.

And then the helicopter lifted free and flew north.

"What was it?" asked Guadalupe Mazatl when she found her voice again.

"It is an evil thing I had thought long dead," intoned the Master of Sinanju bitterly. He watched the bright dragonfly that was the late Comandante Odio's helicopter disappear beyond the drab gray slab of new brutalism architecture that was the Hotel Nikko.

20

Bill Holland listened mesmerized to the cockpit voice recorder.

It was, first of all, amazing that the CVR had even survived the crash. *Air Force One*'s wreckage had been extracted from the sierra by helicopter skycrane and taken to a warehouse in Tampico for preliminary analysis and final extraction of the flight crew, who were inextricably mingled with the compacted cockpit.

It was in the course of that messy task that the CVR was uncovered, dented, but its tape loop intact.

Bill Holland personally flew it back to Washington for analysis.

He hit the rewind button and settled back in the cherrywood conference room at the National Transportation Safety Board headquarters in Washington.

"It doesn't make sense," a voice was saying. It was the human-factors expert.

"We can account for it," Holland said in a testy voice. "Let's just listen again."

He found the point on the tape just before impact and let the tape run.

The voices of the flight crew were tense. The pilot was saying, "It's like she's trying to save herself."

The copilot's voice came on then, controlled, only slightly warped by concern. It might have been a defect in the tape and not his voice. They were a professional crew.

"We've lost the other engines."

"We're going in. Dump the fuel."

"Oh, my God. Look. She's already dumping! It's like she can read our minds."

"That explains why there was no fire," the human-factors expert said.

Then it came. The long scream of metal as the underbelly was ripped along the desert floor. A pop. A hissing as the air rushed out of the still-pressurized cabin. Familiar sounds.

The sound of impact, when it came, was terrible. It was like a trash compactor crushing apple crates. It went on for a long time and Holland's mind flashed back to his first aerial view of that long imprint in the desert. He shivered.

It ended with a crump of a sound that mingled with the crunching of the windscreen against the base of the mountain.

Then silence.

Normally the tape would stop with the disruption of electrical power. But somehow this tape jerked on.

And somewhere in the cockpit, the crushed cockpit containing what was later determined to be completely dismembered bodies, a high metallic voice squealed: "*Survive . . . survive . . . survive . . . must survive.*"

"It doesn't sound human," the human-factors guy said.

"It's definitely a voice," Holland retorted. He took a sip of his coffee. Stone cold. He finished it anyway.

"Transmission?" a voice offered.

"The radio was destroyed upon impact," Holland said. "That was a member of the flight crew. Who else could it have been?"

No one knew. And so they listened to the tape once again, and on into the afternoon, attempting to explain the inexplicable.

Finally they decided that it was a freak of electronics. The CVR tape overwrote the loop every thirty minutes. The squealing voice repeating "survive" had not been recorded after impact, but was the garbled residue of previously overwritten recording.

"Are we all agreed on this?" Bill Holland asked wearily.

Heads nodded. But no face bore a look of conviction. But in the face of the impossible, it was the best explanation they had. There were already too many other anomalies. The gunshot wounds. The eyeless, toothless skull. The missing heads. The still-missing presidential body. No one wanted to add more to the list.

"Then that's it," Holland said. "Let's move on."

The official NTSB preliminary report on SAM 2700 was rushed through channels. Within an hour, it had been messengered to the FBI, the State Department, and the White House. Not everyone who read this "For Your Eyes Only" copy knew that SAM 2700 was the official designation for *Air Force One*.

One person who did not know was an FBI file clerk named Fred Skilicorn. A copy of the file ended up in his hands after it had been received at FBI headquarters in Washington. He had it for only ten minutes. That was enough time for him to skim it and, after delivering it to his superior, make a surreptitious phone call.

Fred Skilicorn officially worked for the FBI. But the extra check that landed in his post-office box every month bore the CIA shield. The CIA knew nothing about the check, however. It was drawn off a secret CURE payroll. Many people worked for CURE. Most of them—like Fred Skilicorn—never knew it.

It was Fred Skilicorn's job to leak sensitive FBI intelligence to the rival CIA. Or so he thought.

The number he called was a recorded message identified only by its phone number. Skilicorn whispered a quick gist of the NTSB report and hung up.

Within seconds the audio recording was electronically converted into print copy and squirted over the telephone lines to a very active computer at Folcroft Sanitarium, where Dr. Harold W. Smith was doggedly tracking all message traffic in and out of Washington, D.C. The town was like a pressure cooker about to blow its lid. Rumors were flying. The president was overdue in Bogotá. The press were told his plane had laid over in Acapulco. Authorities in Acapulco denied the story. The story was hastily revised to a Panama layover. U.S. occupation forces in Panama City issued a clipped "No comment" to every media inquiry and the media was momentarily stymied.

Smith detected only a feeling of unease. There were reports of a major speech to be delivered by the Vice-President. Officially, it was tied in with the President's trip. Unofficially, there were a thousand unconfirmable rumors. Smith was picking up anonymous tips that it was much more than that.

He sweated as he scanned these rumors reaching him. They ran the gamut from the Vice-President's intended divorce to his impending resignation for medical reasons. The resignation story was the one most rife. And it was coming from credible sources at State, from Treasury, and out of the White House itself.

Nothing was breaking in the media. The noon news broadcasts had come and gone, but the evening newscasts were being prepared. And there was no story to report. No arrival of *Air Force One*. Reporters were burning up the phone lines with questions.

And there were no answers.

A blinking screen light warned Smith of an informant's tip emanating from Washington. Smith keyed into it. The gist was brief. Smith absorbed it at a glance.

It was an NTSB preliminary report. He almost dismissed it. What had happened to *Air Force One* would be a matter for tomorrow. The President's fate was today's crisis.

And then Smith saw the remarks about the cockpit voice recorder's final recording. A strange voice that said over and over: "Survive . . . survive . . . must survive."

And Dr. Harold W. Smith's grayish visage paled three times, each time losing another shade of gray.

He sat at his terminal, white as the proverbial ghost. Because what he was reading told him that a ghost from CURE's past had returned—a ghost of plastic and aluminum and fiber optics.

A ghost named Mr. Gordons.

Smith reached for the telephone and began dialing Mexico City. His fingers kept hitting the wrong buttons. He hung up, took a deep breath, and tried again.

21

Remo Williams began to appreciate the size of Chapultepec Park after he had been walking along a winding pathway between bands of ancient cypress trees for twenty minutes and saw no sign of the other side.

It was vast. Like New York's Central Park squared. Sad-faced Mexicans of all varieties, from prosperous businessmen to blanket-clad Indians selling tortillas and *refrescos* from little wheeled carts, milled about. There were so many people roaming the park, Remo wondered if it was some kind of Mexican holiday.

So many people that it was difficult to move quickly through them and impossible to spot the Vice-President—if in fact he were mingling with the jostling crowd.

Remo looked around for someone who might speak English. He spotted a well-dressed blond woman feeding ducks in a pool so large it might pass for a small lake, and worked his way toward her.

"Excuse me," Remo began.

"*Sí?*" the woman asked in Spanish. She turned around and Remo saw the caramel coloring of her smooth skin. He realized her hair had been dyed.

"Habla inglés?" Remo asked.

The woman shook her head, murmuring, "No *inglés*. Sorry."

"Thanks anyway." Remo moved on. His head hurt and he lowered his respiration cycle to keep out the pollutants. Unfortunately, this also decreased the amount of already-sparse oxygen getting to his lungs. The effect was like starving the fire that was the sun source burning deep within his solar plexus, the true seat of his soul, as he had been taught by Chiun.

Another few yards, another blond head bobbed. Remo pushed through the crowd to reach her.

"Excuse me," he called. "Help out a fellow American?"

"I am not an *americana*," she replied.

"But you *do* speak English," Remo prompted.

"Does it not seem that way to you?" she asked demurely.

"Yeah, yeah," Remo said impatiently. "Look. Have you seen the Vice-President around here?"

"No. Perhaps you should go to the Presidential Palace."

"No. I mean *my* Vice-President."

"Your Vice-President?"

"Yeah. The U.S. Vice-President. *Comprendo?*"

"Comprende," the Mexican blond corrected. "And I do not know what he looks like."

"I thought everyone knew his face."

"You *gringos* are such egotists. Can you tell me what the Mexican Vice-President looks like? Or our President?"

Remo winced. "Point taken," he admitted. "The guy I'm looking for really stands out in a crowd. He's got a golf bag over one shoulder and—"

"Golf? What is golf?"

"It's a game. Played with clubs. You know—fore?"
Remo pantomined Arnold Palmer teeing off. He got
a quizzically raised eyebrow that was twenty shades
darker than the hair above it.

"I am sorry, *señor*. I cannot help you."

Remo started to go, then remembering something.
"How about Robert Redford? See any sign of him?"

"No," the blond said brightly. "Is Señor Redford
in Mexico?"

"I doubt it," Remo said sourly. He stalked away.

He decided that his best bet was to climb one of
the towering cypress trees. He went up the nearest
bole.

By the time he reached the crown, his hands were
dusty with pollution particles that had come off the
leaves and branches like tomb dust.

He looked at his fingertips. The stuff resembled
fine ash, but it gleamed with metallic traces.

"Unbelievable," Remo grumbled. "Even the trees
are dirty." He looked around, stepping from branch
to branch to get different views of the park.

There was no sign of the Vice-President, nor of
anyone carrying a golf bag. Not that even Remo's
sharp eyes could have easily picked one man out of
the teeming throng.

Releasing a defeated sigh, Remo started to climb
down off the tree.

He heard the helicopter before he saw it. The
sound made him jump back to the grass. He looked up.

To the north, a helicopter lifted free of the cypress-
dotted horizon. It vectored away toward the concrete
tower that was the Hotel Nikko.

Remo recognized it as Comandante Odie's personal ship. The markings and mounted machine guns
gave it away.

He started to run back to the Reforma. After his lungs began to burn, he changed his mind and dropped back to a trot.

By the time he reached the exit gate, he was walking.

The Master of Sinanju was waiting impatiently in the brick park where Remo had last seen him.

Remo approached wearing a frown. Something was wrong. He could tell it by the dark expression on his mentor's yellow face. Officer Mazatl was likewise troubled. Her flat eyes were dazed, almost wounded.

"Who took off in the chopper?" Remo asked breathlessly.

"Josip Broz Tito," Guadalupe Mazatl said flatly.

"Who's Josip Broz Tito?" Remo wanted to know.

Lupe pointed to the dais, now empty. Big bronze letters said "JOSIP BROZ TITO," and under that were the dates "1892–1980." He saw the shiny new-penny patches where the statue's feet had been. And it came to him what was wrong. The statue was missing.

"Okay," Remo said. "I have a headache and we're getting nowhere. I see the pedestal and I see that there's no statue there anymore. In twenty-five words or less, what the hell happened?"

"It was Gordons," Chiun said, brittle-voiced.

"*Impossible!*" Remo exploded.

"Who is Gordon?" asked Guadalupe Mazatl.

"Completely impossible!" Remo repeated.

"I spoke with the statue known as Josip Broz Tito," Chiun began.

"Wait a minute—what about the Vice-President?" Remo wanted to know.

"Gordons *is* the Vice-President. Or he was. Now he is this Tito thing."

"Who is this Gordon?" Guadalupe asked again.

Remo snapped at her, "Stay out of this, will you, please!"

"Interventionist *americano*!" Lupe muttered. "Whose country is this, anyhow?" But she shut up. She looked as unsteady as a dandelion in a freshening wind.

"The statue *talked* to you?" Remo asked Chiun.

"Yes. He wished to know why we were pursuing him. I explained this to him. It was then that I recognized the childlike mind of the man-machine Gordons. I was very clever, Remo. I did not let on that I knew he was Gordons, not Tito."

"If it were anybody but that walking GoBot," Remo muttered darkly, "I'd wonder who fooled whom. But Gordons has the reasoning powers of a six-year-old."

"There is more," Chiun added.

"Look, my head is ringing like Quasimodo's bell," Remo complained. "Let's get back to our hotel, where the air isn't carcinogenic and we can talk to Smith. Let him figure this out."

As they turned up the Reforma, Officer Guadalupe Mazatl asked a question:

"Who is Smith?" She pronounced it "Smeeth."

"We do not know anyone named that," Chiun said flatly.

Remo said nothing. He pinched the bridge of his nose, between his closed eyes. They felt like ball bearings.

After a twenty-minute ride during which Remo had personally rolled up every car window, Remo and Chiun were back in their room at the Krystal.

"The first item on the agenda is order room service," Remo said, pushing aside the videotape of the President's rescue to get at the phone. "We haven't eaten since this thing started."

"Yes, food will help you," Lupe said.

Remo got the order clerk. "I'd like two portions of boiled rice. Just the rice. No salt, no pepper. No nothing. Just rice. Better make it two double portions. *Gracias*," he added, using the only word of Spanish he felt sure of.

After he put down the receiver, Remo noticed Guadalupe looking at him with a mixture of wonder and pity.

"What's the matter now?" he demanded.

"I do not understand."

"Join the club," Remo said distractedly. "I thought Gordons was dead for good."

"I do not know this Gordon, but this is not about him."

"About what, then?"

"If neither of you has eaten, how could you suffer from the *turistas*?"

"Is that what they call this bad air-sickness?" Remo asked, throwing himself onto the bed. Chiun lay atop the other one, his eyes closed, his fingers touching his temples. He rubbed them methodically.

"No. That is *la contaminación*. The *turistas* are what you *gringos* call Moctezuma's Revenge."

"Montezuma," Remo corrected.

"I am pure Aztec," Lupe insisted. "It is Moctezuma, no matter what the *ladinos* or *norteamericanos* might say."

"I'll take your word for it," Remo said sourly. "And Montezuma's Revenge isn't what ails us."

"Then why did you order only rice?" Lupe asked, puzzled.

"We always eat rice. It's like spinach to Chiun and me."

"Spinach?"

"You know, Popeye, the Sailor Man."

"Ah, Popeye. But I still do not understand."

"Let's keep it that way." Remo glanced over to the Master of Sinanju. "Okay, Chiun, let's have the sordid details. And talk slowly. I'm going to have to explain this to Smith."

"Gordons is the President of Vice," Chiun said hollowly. "He has been the President of Vice all along. This explains many things, not least the selection of a callow youth as the true President's prince."

"He's not a prince and I don't buy that," Remo retorted. "The Vice-President didn't just pop out of the fifth dimension one day. He has a wife and family. He was a senator for years. No, Gordons may have been impersonating the Vice-President, but he is not the Vice-President. The Vice-President is still in the U.S. Smith said so."

"It is possible Smith is mistaken," Chiun sniffed.

"I doubt it."

"You and I were mistaken. We thought we had destroyed Gordons. Four times we believed this true, and still he returns to trouble our lives."

Remo folded his bare arms in annoyance. "Yeah. That's strange. We know he can be destroyed. All we have to do is wreck his central processor, or whatever it's called. Trouble is, it's not always in the same place. Once it was in his head, and another time in his heel. Last time it was in his left hand."

"No, it was not!" Chiun snapped. "That thing you dismembered last time was not Gordons, but an automaton created by Gordons. His true brain was in the deadly satellite, which I vanquished at the same time you battled the false Gordons."

"No, that was Gordons," Remo said with conviction. "I nailed him. And he went down. End of story."

"I destroyed his brain," Chiun insisted, "and the false Gordons collapsed. It had nothing to do with your blow, ineffectual as it was."

"Wrong."

"Right. I am always right."

Remo sighed. "Listen, I thought we settled this argument."

"We did," Chiun retorted. "I dispatched the true Gordons."

"Yeah?" Remo countered. "Then what is he doing running around Mexico City tricked up to look like the Vice-President?"

"I do not know," Chiun sniffed. "But we can ask him later."

Remo sat up. "We can?"

"I have arranged a meeting with Gordons—the true Gordons—at the place called Teotihuacán. It is there we will negotiate for the safety of the President. And it is there that Gordons will tell you the truth of our last encounter with him."

"I can hardly wait," Remo said sourly. "So what does Gordons want?"

"What Gordons always wants. What he is programmed to want. To survive."

"Right. Survival. The prime directive." Remo's face darkened. "You know, I'm really, really sick of him coming back to haunt us."

The food arrived at that moment. Guadalupe Mazatl, who had been an interested but puzzled listener to the conversation, let the hotel waiter in. She shooed him away with a quick burst of Spanish and a fat tip.

Remo and Chiun got up and attacked the rice. Spurning the wheeled serving cart, they set the silver tray on the rug and assumed lotus positions before it as they dug in.

They ate in silence, and quietly Guadalupe joined them on the floor.

"I have been listening to your conversation," she said tentatively.

"Must be a local custom," Remo grumbled.

They ate with what Guadalupe thought was peculiar intensity, like men about to go into battle.

"I have listened to you discuss this *hombre* Gordon," she persisted. "Sometimes you talk of him as if he were a man. Other times as a machine. Which is it?"

"Both," Remo said.

"Neither," Chiun said.

"I would like to know more about this creature."

"It's our President," Remo said. "And our problem."

"And I will remind you that this is my country," Guadalupe replied tartly. "I am a law-enforcement officer. It is my duty to deal with internal threats."

"Tough," Remo said through a mouthful of rice.

"Tell her, Remo," Chiun said suddenly.

"Why?"

"Because I am eating and I would rather suffer through your words than her nagging."

"What is 'nagging'?" Lupe demanded.

"What you were just doing," Chiun replied. "Remo."

Remo put down his rice. "All right," he began. "Years ago there was this crazy female NASA scientist. She liked to drink and she liked to make robots almost as much. Her dream was to create a thinking robot to send on long-distance space flights. Instead of sending people, NASA would send robots. Or androids. I guess Gordons is an android."

"I know this word 'robot,' but not 'android,'" Lupe admitted.

"It's like a robot, except it looks and acts almost human," Remo explained. "Kinda like Arnold Schwarzenegger. Well, this woman scientist invented Mr. Gordons. This was after Mr. Seagrams and Mr. Smirnoff didn't work out."

"Those are liquor brands," Guadalupe said doubtfully.

"Didn't I mention she liked to drink? Well, that's what too much Gordon's gin will do for you. Gordons walks and talks like a man. He thinks like a six-year-old. But he knows how to do one thing well—survive. That's what he's programmed to do, and that's what he does."

"Survive . . . ?" Lupe repeated.

Remo nodded. "Survive. That's where the real trouble with Gordons all began. When NASA funding was curtailed back in the seventies, the Gordons project was defunded. Gordons figured he'd be turned off, so he escaped. He's been on the loose ever since."

"He is a menace?"

"Menace and a half," Remo said ruefully. "For a guy who's only interest is getting through the day, he's caused a junkyard's worth of trouble. We chased him to hell and gone in the U.S., all the way to Moscow, where the Russians shot him into space. We thought that was finally the end of him. He came back as a Russian space shuttle, later turning up, variously, as a car-wash machine and an amusement park."

"You are making no sense," Lupe said.

Remo snapped his fingers. "Right. I forgot a step. Gordons is an assimilator. He assimilates things in order to survive. That means he becomes them. Any object, inanimate or living, that he can get his plastic

hooks into—bingo, it becomes Gordons. That's how
he was able to look like the Vice-President. That's
how he survived falling sixteen stories. He's self-
repairing. He just picked himself up and lit off. He
must have become the statue of Tito as camouflage."

"This is an incredible story—too incredible to be
believed."

"We've got Gordons as the Vice-President on that
videotape over there," Remo said, jerking a thumb
back to a nightstand. "And you were the one who
talked to Tito, not me."

Lupe closed her eyes. "I still shake when I hear
that statue speak in my mind," she said hollowly.

"Wish I'd been there," Remo said fiercely, picking
at his rice. "I would have ripped his head off."

"And the secret of the true President's fate would
have perished with him," Chiun pointed out. "Unless his brain is in his little toe this time, in which
case your attack would have been for nothing."

"Touché," Remo said. And seeing Guadalupe's puzzled brows knit together, added, "It's French."

"Meaning what?"

"Search me," Remo said.

"You want me to search you? What will I find?"

Remo closed his eyes. "Never mind. Look, we've
only got another couple of hours before we go to . . .
What is it called again?"

"Teotihuacán. It is a ruin."

"Unlike Mexico City, which is only a disaster,"
Remo muttered. "Right. So we've got to get orders
from home."

"From Smith?"

"We don't know any Smeeth," Remo said blandly.

"You are making fun of me," Guadalupe accused.
She pronounced it "fon."

"Anyway, we have to make a private phone call," Remo continued. "Mind waiting outside until we call you back in?"

"We who are working together should have no secrets. May I stay?"

"Can you say 'juniper juice jelly is yummy' three times fast without making a mistake?" Remo asked.

Guadalupe got to her feet stiffly. Such rudeness, she thought. These Americans ordered people around in their own nation like they were the landlords of the earth.

"Yust as you say," she said with studied formality, "I will go." She backed away from them, plucking the videotape off the nightstand while they were engrossed in their rice.

She left the room without another word.

After the door shut behind her, Remo finished the last of his rice, washing it down with mineral water.

"She is not coming back, you know," Chiun said pointedly.

"Better for us. Better for her," Remo said, reaching up for the telephone. He wondered how Smith would take the news.

22

Jorge Chingar, alias El Padrino, arrived in Mexico City in a Lear private jet that was waved to a private hangar by the ground crew.

Mexican customs inspectors were already waiting for him as the hatch of his Lear dropped, revealing the lambskin-carpeted steps on its underside.

El Padrino stepped off the plane, grinning darkly.

"Buenos días, muchachos," he cried, flinging out his arms grandly.

He came off the plane before his personal guard. Although he was a wanted man back in Colombia, and technically here in Mexico, El Padrino was unafraid.

The customs officers stepped forward, their faces very serious, as is the way of customs men the world over.

"Have you anything to declare, *señor?*" one asked.

"Any weapons? Any drugs? Any illegal contraband?" asked the others.

El Padrino reached into his silk Versace jacket, extracted an alligator-skin wallet, and began peeling off American hundred-dollar bills.

He presented two to each of the customs men and then handed the leader a sealed envelope.

"For your *amigos*," he said graciously.

"*Muy bien, señor*," said the chief customs officer.

They nodded their heads politely and, their duty fulfilled, left the hangar.

El Padrino clapped his bejeweled fingers, bringing his personal guard.

They came carrying weapons and looking fierce.

"Guard the plane. No one comes in or out. You cannot trust these Mexicans, no matter how much you pay them."

His men deployed around the hangar with military precision, as well they should. They had been trained by Israeli mercenaries.

El Padrino turned on his heel and reentered the cabin. In his private cabin he worked the phone.

El Padrino played the telephone like a master musician, his voice smooth almost to the point of unctuousness. He never overdid it. And so received quick polite answers.

But they were not answers he liked. Comandante Odio was dead, the DFS told him. It was most regrettable. No, there were no further details available at this time.

"This is unfortunate," said El Padrino to the *primer comandante* of the DFS. "Comandante Odio was a very valuable man. I fear I cannot replace a man so valuable as he."

"Perhaps we could work something out," suggested the *primer comandante*.

"Ah, I was hoping you would say that," said El Padrino, who understood that in Mexico, at least, money did not talk. It beguiled.

"If you would like to discuss this further, you may come to my office," the *primer comandante* was saying.

"I would much prefer that you experience the

hospitality of my fine aircraft. The wines are French and the food is Andalusian."

"I shall join you directly," said the *primer comandante*. The phone went *click*.

Yes, thought El Padrino. These Mexicans were so very easy to do business with. Perhaps in a few years, if business continued to expand, he would move his operation to Mexico City. Colombia was more refined, but the government very, very entrenched. In Mexico they were more flexible. They even had a saying that governed their code of behavior: "Money does not stink."

El Padrino snapped his fingers and a steward entered the cabin.

"Prepare on excellent meal," El Padrino instructed. "We are having important guests. And see how the *presidente*'s quarters are coming. I wish him to enjoy every civilized comfort during his journey to Colombia."

"*Sí,*" Padrino."

23

Remo Williams noticed the missing videotape as he reached for the phone. It rang before he could ask Chiun about it. Frowning, he brought the receiver to his mouth.

It was Smith. "Remo!" he said tensely. "I've been trying to get you for hours!"

"We've been out working, remember?" Remo reminded him.

"Did you get any of my messages?"

"What messages?" Remo demanded.

"I left nearly a dozen. My God, didn't the front desk give them to you?"

"Smitty, you have a lot to learn about the way they do things down here," Remo said. "Look, we've got bad news. I hope you're sitting down."

"It's Gordons, isn't it?" Smith asked.

"How'd you know that!" Remo blurted.

"His voice was recorded by *Air Force One*'s flight data recorder," Smith said testily, "but never mind that. Time is of the essence. Give me your report."

"The short version is: the guy running around pretending to be the Vice-President is Gordons," Remo said.

"You encountered him?"

"Yeah, but he slipped away. Last seen resembling Josip Broz Tito dipped in bronze."

"Beg pardon?"

"Read about it in my memoirs," Remo said glumly. "Let's stay on track here. We have only two hours. Gordons has set up a meet. He has some crazy idea that the President's survival is linked to his. He's willing to hand him over in return for certain guarantees."

"We cannot trust that man—I mean, machine."

"I know what you mean, but Chiun has him thinking we don't know who he is. If Chiun is right—"

"I am," Chiun said loudly enough for Smith to hear. "I never fail. When I have been sent to the proper place at the proper time. Unlike this mission."

"If Chiun's right," Remo went on, "Gordons may come along peacefully. Maybe we can make this work. Once we have the President, dealing with Gordons will be another matter."

"What does Gordons want?"

"Hard to say," Remo said. "Safe passage to the U.S. Diplomatic immunity. Fifty cases of Three-in-One oil. With that ambulatory junk pile, who the hell knows? I say we give him what he wants and sort out the casualties after the President is safe."

"Yes. Absolutely. Do what you have to, Remo. Offer him anything. Just bring the President back alive."

"Just call me Frank Buck," Remo said. "You know," he added, "I can't believe this. How the hell did Gordons get involved in this?"

Smith expelled air into his receiver. "I did some backtracking, Remo," he said wearily. "You remember that Gordons had taken over that California theme park, Larryland."

"I remember it, well," Remo said. "He had the place rigged with that stolen Russian satellite, the one that sterilized people with microwave bursts. He thought he'd sterilize every visitor and eventually wipe out the human race. We'd all die out and he'd survive. Him and the cockroaches."

"The Army Corps of Engineers blew up Larryland."

"I was there too. I thought Gordons was gone for good."

"As it happens, the previous President had been flying to his California ranch during that operation," Smith said. "*Air Force One* flew over the detonation site, apparently on orders from the President, who wanted to see the explosion from the air."

"What?"

"This is supposition," Smith went on, "but if Gordons' central processor survived the explosion, it could have been exploded upward, possibly high enough to attach itself to *Air Force One*."

"Christ!" Remo rasped. "You mean Gordons *became Air Force One*?"

"It is my best guess," Smith admitted.

"And two presidents have been riding around inside him?"

"It is a sobering thought, I know," Smith admitted.

"Sobering? It makes my blood run cold. What was he up to?"

"Think about it, Remo. Gordons exists to survive, and survives to exist. *Air Force One* has an excellent maintenance program and relatively light duty cycles. Gordons is a machine. As *Air Force One*, he would be the most pampered machine on earth. No one suspected him. No one molested him. In a way, it's unfortunate that this happened the way it did. The presidential plane is scheduled to be replaced in

another year. Gordons would have been retired from
service."

"We gotta nail him this time," Remo said fiercely.

"No. The President comes first. Gordons is sec-
ondary."

"What happened to acing the President if he com-
promises national security?" Remo asked.

There was silence on the line. Remo started to
say, "Hello?"

Smith spoke. "If anything goes wrong, that is your
option of last resort. Some things are going on in
Washington I do not understand, but we have an
extremely sensitive political situation developing."

"Tell me about it," Remo sighed, a vision of the
Vice-President—the real one—floating through his
mind. "Look, one way or another, we should have
this wrapped up tonight. Will the lid stay on that
long?"

"Barely. The media are getting restive. Report
back as soon as the situation is resolved."

"Gotcha."

Remo hung up. He turned to Chiun. "We're a go
for negotiating. But Smith says if it goes bad, the
President is better off dead."

The Master of Sinanju's tired eyebrows lifted. "Ah,
he is preparing to make his move at last."

"No. It's a last resort."

"Smith is clever," Chiun mused. "Perhaps this
entire scheme is his doing."

Remo went to the door and looked out in the
hallway. There was no sign of Guadalupe Mazatl. He
shut the door.

"You were right," he told Chiun. "Lupe's cut out
on us."

"If I was right about one matter, I might be right

about another," Chiun said, getting up. He lifted to his feet like a column of scarlet smoke emerging from a floor heat register.

"Not about that," Remo said flatly. "What do you say we get to Teotihuacán early? Just in case."

"We risk much, the longer we breathe this foul air," Chiun warned.

"I'm feeling better," Remo said, rotating his thick wrists like an arm wrestler warming up.

Chiun nodded. "Now. Here. In this air-conditioned room within our bellies full of rice. But out there, the very air robs us of our strength, our mighty resources. Ordinarily, Gordons is a formidable foe. Under these circumstances, we are as ordinary men."

"So what do you suggest?" Remo wondered.

Chiun raised a lecturing finger. "We avoid combat at all costs. We negotiate, as Smith would have us do."

"Sounds reasonable to me," Remo admitted.

"And then, once back in the pure clean air of America, we will strike, for Gordons has cost us dearly in the past. He murdered the woman you knew as Anna and he robbed me of the seed of the future."

Remo's face grew sad. "Yeah, Anna. Funny, I hadn't thought of her in a long time. And Gordons did sterilize you that last time, didn't he?"

"We have much to repay Gordons for," Chiun said in a cold voice. "But we will do this in the time and place of our own choosing."

24

Behind the pond-scum-brown smog that hung over the Valley of Mexico, the sun set like a smoky brazier. The stagnant air, fed by unregulated car exhausts and industrial smokestacks, stank of carbon dioxide. Millions of pairs of sore human lungs sucked in the unhealthy air. It scoured sinus passages and caused spontaneous nosebleeds. Scarlet tanagers, one moment winging past the Pemex Towers, simply folded their wings and plummeted to their deaths, their immune systems succumbing to toxic chromium levels.

It was just another afternoon in Mexico City.

Except for a series of seemingly unrelated events.

First, the President of the United States woke up to total darkness. He thought he was dreaming. Then he wondered if he were dead. He was not lying down, not standing, but somehow suspended in the dark. His questing fingers brushed an abrasive surface like raw plaster. He found that he could move his arms, but not much. He couldn't move his legs at all. And something was digging into his crotch, on which he was somehow balanced.

His legs tingled with pins and needles. And he

smelled something odd. It reminded him of the stuffed-animal section of the Smithsonian Institution—formaldehyde and dead fur.

He called for help. There was no answer.

The Museum of Anthropology on the Paseo de la Reforma was closed on Mondays. Today was Monday. And so the spacious museum was deserted except for a single guard named Umberto Zamora.

Zamora was making his rounds when he heard the sudden awful grinding sound. Like a million giant pestles grinding maize. He ran to the sound, or where he thought the sound emanated. It changed from the grinding and sparking of stone to a slow, ponderous tread.

Zamora stopped so swiftly he skidded on the polished marble floor. He listened fearfully. The ponderous tread was coming in his direction. Slowly, methodically, unstoppably.

Umberto Zamora felt the floor tremble under his feet, and his courage deserted him. He dived behind a Mayan stela.

There he huddled, trembling as the terrible tread lumbered past him. It was like an earthquake on legs. He waited until it was gone, presumably from the museum—if the terrible rending of wood and metal meant what Zamora thought it meant.

Gingerly Umberto Zamora emerged from hiding. He followed the scuffed floor prints. They led to a hole in one wall. A very big hole. And out on the grass, giant footprints led away.

Off in the grass, an olive helicopter lifted off with difficulty.

Zamora retraced the footprints back into the museum. They ended at the open spot where the statue of the Aztec goddess Coatlicue—She of the Serpent Skirts—had stood for many years. She stood there no longer.

Umberto Zamora was of mostly Mixtec blood. He believed in the old ways. He believed that Quetzalcoatl would one day return to Mexico. Still, he was quite astonished that Coatlicue had stridden away. She was over eight feet tall and made entirely of rude, immobile stone. He noticed the tiny rocky fragments littering the floor, as if Coatlicue had simply shrugged them off.

Then he fell to his knees and began praying to his gods. The old gods. The true gods of Mexico.

Federal Judicial Police Officer Guadalupe Mazatl left the Hotel Krystal in a huff, muttering, "Fock all gringos!"

She was fed up with all gringos. She was sick of the lazy FJP and the corrupt DFS, of every criollo and mestizo who gave in with fatalistic surrender to life's many indignities.

When Officer Mazatl had first joined the FJP, she was determined to be different, not to take bribes or to grovel before the white Mexicans, but to live as an Aztec woman, proud and unbending of spirit.

She had never bent. And as a consequence, she had never been accepted by the mestizo men who complimented her body but secretly yearned for that ultimate Mexican status symbol, a blond woman. In four years with the FJP, she had never advanced beyond officer, and she knew she never would.

But she had retained her self-respect. It was victory enough.

She entered her official vehicle, pride like a mask of her wide brown face, and started the engine.

There was no point in taking this matter to her
primer comandante, that *cabrón*. The DFS would be
of no help either. She had virtually been an accom-
plice to the death of Comandante Odio and his men.
How could she have been so stupid as to get mixed
up with *gringos*? she wondered.

Officer Guadalupe Mazatl decided that if she was
to protect Mexico—the Mexico she both loved and
despised—she must go to Teotihuacán.

She pulled out onto Liverpool, turned right on
Florencia, past the ridiculous Banana boutique with
its King Kong roof diorama which symbolized how
far Mexico had sunk into carnival absurdity, and sent
the car speeding along the Paseo de la Reforma.

Near the María Isabel Sheraton, a DFA vehicle
pulled in front of her. It slowed down, forcing her to
do likewise. Another DFS car appeared on her left.
And a third on her right. They drove in formation
until they reached a red light.

There, DFS agents piled out and demanded she
surrender her weapon. Officer Guadalupe Mazatl knew
better than to refuse.

"What is this about?" she asked as she handed
over her sidearm, holster and all.

"You are under arrest for suspicion of complicity in
the murder of DFS Comandante Oscar Odio," one
agent said. "You will come with us, Officer."

As obligingly as any meek *mestizo*, Officer Mazatl
allowed herself to be bundled into one of the DFS
cars.

"DFS headquarters is not this way," she said when
the cars turned onto Viaducto.

"We are going to the airport," the driver informed
her.

Puzzled, Officer Mazatl folded her strong arms,

wondering why. She decided not to ask. Her Indian fatalism had completely reasserted itself. She despised the feeling.

Remo Williams got lost in the congested Mexico City traffic. He stopped in an area of run-down buildings. He kept every window sealed tight. Still, carbon dioxide was coming up through the VW Beetle's leaky floorboards.

"Damn this rental car," he told Chiun. "Remind me to slaughter that desk clerk who arranged this."

"I will leave you what still quivers," the Master of Sinanju said. He breathed through a scarlet kimono sleeve held over his nose.

Remo spotted a Mexico City traffic cop astride a motorcycle parked in a no-parking zone. As much as he hated to roll down the window, he did. Being lost in Mexican traffic hell was infinitely worse.

"Hey!" he called over. "Point me to Teotihuacán?"

The traffic cop put a hand to his ear. "*Qué?*"

"Teotihuacán," Remo repeated. "*Comprende?*"

"Ah, come closer, *señor.*"

Remo sent his car closer to the white-lined zone where the officer was parked.

"Closer, *señor,*" the cop repeated.

"Teotihuacán," Remo said.

"Closer," the cop said, wiggling his fingers invitingly.

And when Remo had the car nose-to-nose with the motorcycle, the officer dismounted, pulled out a ticket pad, and said, "Oh, *señor,* you have crossed the white line. Now I must give you a ticket."

Remo looked down. His front tire barely touched the white no-parking line.

"But you told me to come closer!" he protested.

"But I did not give permission to cross the white line, *señor.*"

Remo got out of the car. He ripped the ticket pad from the man's hands, tore his gunbelt free, and as a final expression of displeasure, stomped the motorcycle into an agony of spare parts.

"Teotihuacán, *señor?*" the cop said quickly. "Go *norte.*"

"Point," Remo said. "I forgot my compass."

The suddenly smiling traffic cop obliged. Remo said *gracias* in a metallic voice and got back into the car.

Twenty minutes later, they were driving past a cemetery set in the foothills of one of Mexico City's towering sentinel mountains. One side of the mountain was a beehive of tar-paper and cardboard shacks, set cheek by jowl.

"I can't believe people live like this," Remo muttered.

Past the mountains, the terrain flattened and was dotted with feathery trees and the occasional rose-pink chapel. The air became cleaner. But not clean enough to induce Chiun to breathe it directly. Remo's head was pounding now. It was still like breathing unadulterated car exhaust. The pit of his stomach felt cold, like a spent coal.

"How do you feel, Little Father?" he asked.

"Ill," Chiun croaked through his sleeve.

"Wonderful," he muttered, noticing the sign that said SAN JUAN TEOTIHUACÁN. "We're walking into one on the worst situations in our lives and we're freaking basket cases."

"We are Sinanju," Chiun said wearily. "And we will prevail." Then he coughed. Remo had never heard his mentor cough before, and it frightened him.

25

The question was put to Officer Guadalupe Mazatl by the fat man the others called, with slimy deference, "El Padrino."

"Qué quieres? Plata, o plomo?" In English: "What do you want? Silver, or lead?"

DFS Primer Comandante Embutes held a Glock pistol to Guadalupe's smooth brown forehead. She knelt before El Padrino, her eyes more shamed than frightened. It was the question she had dreaded back in Tampico. The *narco-traficantes* would give other FJP officers the same choice: accept bribes and look the other way, or die.

Guadalupe's lower lip trembled. She had thought she knew what her answer would be. But she was without a pistol now. And as El Padrino, who was dressed like an Acapulco gigolo, looked at her with feigned indifference, she muttered the word that tasted of bitterness.

"Plata," she said, adding, *"No me mates, por favor."* The pistol was withdrawn.

Comandante Embutes said, "Very wise, *señorita*. Now you will tell us all about the *americanos*, and their *presidente*."

The words tumbled out of Guadalupe's Mazatl's mouth. She told them everything, about the false Vice-President, about the speaking statue. They scoffed at first, but when she produced the videotape, they scoffed no longer.

El Padrino's video machine played the scene over and over in the plush stateroom of his Lear jet. The cabin was very silent except for muttered curses.

"Josip Broz Tito, eh?" El Padrino said finally, turning to her. "Tito was a good man. Perhaps we can bargain with him, eh?"

"He wants only to survive," Guadalupe muttered abjectly. "That is what the *gringos* have said. To survive."

El Padrino stood up. He nodded to Comandante Embutes. He pulled Guadalupe to her feet, checking the cords that bound her hands behind her back.

El Padrino lifted her chin in his many-ringed hands.

"We all wish to survive, eh, *chica?*"

And Officer Guadalupe Mazatl lowered her head in Aztec shame at his arrogant *ladino* smile.

26

Remo parked at the tourist entrance to the ruined necropolis of Teotihuacán. There was a museum ticket booth nearby. The door stood open. It was deserted.

"Looks like everybody cleared out," Remo said, coming out of the museum. He handed the Master of Sinanju a brochure, saying, "Here's a layout of the place, in case we have to split up."

They walked between two long buildings into the ruins, coming to the base of an immense flat-sided pyramid that reared up for hundreds of feet so steeply its summit could not be seen. It was like a square wedding cake, each section smaller than the one under it. The broad stairs stopped at frequent open terraces.

"Remo, such magnificence!" Chiun squeaked suddenly, his tired eyes brightening to birdlike clarity.

"It's the Pyramid of the Sun," Remo replied. "And don't get carried away with past glories. The Aztecs are all gone."

"It looks almost Egyptian. Could these Aztecs have been a colony of Egypt? Only the Pyramid of Cheops rivals this."

Remo frowned. They were standing on a long

straight stone-paved road. Grass grew in the chinks between the cobbles. In fact, it grew along the sides of the dull brown pyramid.

"Says here we're standing on the Avenue of the Dead," Remo said, reading from his brochure. He gazed down the road. Past a line of flat structures like flat-topped temples, the road ended at the foot of a smaller pyramid that seemed to have been excavated from a hill. The back of the pyramid was still embedded in the hill.

"And that's the Pyramid of the Moon," Remo added. He looked up. "I didn't expect anything this big. There's an awful lot of ground to cover. What do you think?"

"I think that we missed a wonderful client in the Aztecs," Chiun said wistfully, scanning his brochure.

"Forget that stuff," Remo snapped. "We'd better get organized before Gordons gets here." He looked up. "What about the top of this pyramid?"

The Master of Sinanju shaded his eyes, trying to see the pyramid's top. He could not.

"Yes," he said. "We will go up this one."

They started up the tumbledown steps. The stairs became broader as they ascended, until they reached the middle terrace, where they paused to look around and catch their breath.

"Better watch it, Little Father," Remo warned. "You can't see the steps until you're on top of them. Don't walk off the side."

The Master of Sinanju stepped to the terrace lip and looked down. It was true. The broken stone steps were so steep one had to walk to the very edge before they became visible. He frowned. The mighty Egyptians had never constructed anything so marvelous.

The city of Teotihuacán extended for several square miles in every direction. Despite the danger, Remo was impressed by its sad vastness. "I wonder if America will ever reach this stage?" he wondered aloud.

"Count on it," Chiun said. "Let us continue."

They trudged up to the topmost terrace, their lungs laboring to extract oxygen from the thin, polluted air. Chiun's breath whistled.

Above them, the pyramid's apex was accessible by a narrow flight of steps so steep that it was impossible to see their top. They seemed to merge with the brownish sky.

Remo was looking down toward a distant stone edifice his brochure called the Temple of Quetzalcoatl. "I don't see any sign of Tito," he said. "Guess we gotta go to the top."

They started the final ascent. As they mounted the rubble-strewn steps, a towering stone carving became visible. It stood amid the rocks of the pyramid's uneven summit.

Remo looked at it without pleasure. "What the hell is this thing?"

It stood over eight feet in height, and seemed almost four feet wide. It was made of rude stone. It resembled, if anything, an Aztec conception of a robot. The broad head was carved into serpent heads perched nose-to-nose so that its side-mounted orbs looked out with wall-eyed balefulness. It wore a ghoulish double grin. Two other serpent heads formed shoulder epaulets, and instead of hands it sported blunted stone slabs. Its chest was arrayed with human hearts and dismembered hands. A skull served as a kind of belt buckle.

There was barely enough room on the rubble-strewn top for them and the idol when they joined it on the summit.

"It is an ugly Aztec goddess," Chiun said, looking around at the panorama of dead Teotihuacán far below. A river meandered nearby, as brown as an earthworn.

"I think you're right," Remo said, examining the idol. "It's a female. That's a skirt made of snakes. The whole thing is a walking snake pit." He paged through his brochure, trying find the snake goddess's name.

"I do not see any sign of Tito below," Chiun said, looking west.

"Ugly monstrosity, isn't it?" Remo muttered, looking at the idol's clawed feet. "Not exactly Egyptian."

"Its head is two serpents joined at the nose," Chiun noted. "The Egyptian gods had animal heads too."

"If this is Egyptian, I'm as Aztec as Guadalupe."

"Behold," Chiun said suddenly, pointing to a cleared area of dirt where sat an olive helicopter. Comandante Odio's helicopter. Remo saw that the front seats were mangled and mashed.

Remo looked up. "He's already here," he said grimly. "Damn!"

"Beware, Remo," Chiun intoned. "He was not in the form of Tito when he journeyed here. He was much larger, much heavier. For both seats are crushed."

"Good. That'll make him easier to spot," Remo said. He turned his attention back to the brochure. "Funny," he muttered. "I can't find it."

"Keep looking," Chiun said, his keen eyes raking the surrounding terrain. "He must be somewhere."

"Not Tito. This stone thing. According to this,

we're standing on the rubble of a temple. No mention of any snake goddess," Remo's voice got smaller. "Uh-oh," he muttered, his gaze lifting to the double serpent head. He eyed its blank scaly face for expression.

"Little Father," he said softly.

The Master of Sinanju turned, his eyes quizzical. He saw his pupil's thumb surreptitiously jerking in the direction of the stone snake idol.

Chiun's eyes went very wide. Then, in a high squeaky voice, he said, "I hope our friend Josip Broz Tito arrives very soon."

"Yes indeedy," Remo chimed in brightly, edging away from the massive idol. "Be nice if he's early. The plane is waiting to take us back to the U.S., where we'll all be nice and safe."

"True, true," Chiun rejoined, also stepping away from the idol. "There is no telling what will happen to him if these Mexicans discover he has usurped their precious statue. He will be in very grave danger. They are no doubt pursuing him mightily at this very moment."

"Hope nothing happens," Remo added loudly. "I'd sure like to help him out."

They stopped. The statue simply stood there, immobile, invincible, inert. An Aztec golem.

"Maybe they already got him," Remo ventured pointedly.

"Yes, you are undoubtedly correct, Remo," Chiun said. "Let us go. There is nothing we can do for poor Tito now."

They started down the steps.

The sudden sound was like breaking rocks. It came from the summit. They turned, their hands lifting defensively, ready for anything.

The stone idol called Coatlicue roused to life. The kissing serpents parted and pointed down at them, a double-headed monstrosity on weaving stone necks. Its arms lifted to show its maimed forearms. And it spoke in a voice like grinding stones.

"*I am here!*" he rumbled.

"You are no longer Tito," Chiun remarked calmly.

"*I can assume whatever shape I desire.*"

"We are pleased to meet you again, O statue," Chiun called up. "For we have come to parley."

The idol stepped forward on its clawed feet. Both heads looked at Remo. "*And you?*"

"We're both ready to negotiate," Remo said.

"*Very well. I will surrender your President on two conditions.*"

Chiun smiled thinly. "Name them."

"*One. That we are taken to a place of safety.*"

"Done," said the Master of Sinanju.

"*Two. That I take the place of one who holds a position of security in the President's government.*"

"Tito's dead," Remo called, "and he's not with our government."

"*I mean the meat machine you call Vice-President of the United States.*"

Remo's eyes went wide. Chiun's narrowed.

"Why would you want that?" Remo wondered sincerely.

"*I understand his duties are undemanding. I understand that he is well-paid, well-protected, and has much leisure time.*"

"You understand right," Remo said.

"*These are my conditions. I am prepared to assume the form of the Vice-President at any time. I pledge to serve the office well, asking only to be unmolested for the natural span of my lifetime.*"

Remo and Chiun exchanged glances.

"Couldn't be any worse than the VP we already have," Remo muttered.

They turned to Coatlicue's wavering stone serpent regard.

"It's a deal," Remo said, poker-faced. "Now that that's settled, where are you keeping the President?"

The stone serpent heads opened their dry cold mouths to answer.

From far below came the sound of car engines and slamming doors. Feet scraped on rocks.

Remo whirled. Racing across the Avenue of the Dead came Officer Guadalupe Mazatl and a host of men he had never seen. Armed men. One in a blue DFS uniform. He was pulling Guadalupe along.

"*Who are those meat machines?*" rumbled the idol who was Mr. Gordons.

"Search me," Remo mumbled.

"*Why should I search you?*"

"Just an expression," Remo said quickly. "They're not with us. Honest."

"Is this a trap?" asked Mr. Gordons in a flinty voice.

"Of course not," Remo said quickly. "Is it, Chiun?"

"No, it is not a trap," the Master of Sinanju snapped. "We have nothing to do with these people."

"*I recognize the female meat machine. She accompanied the old one before.*"

"But she's not with us anymore," Remo said quickly. "I don't know what's going on."

The contingent of men came up the steps huffing and puffing.

A voice called out. Guadalupe's.

"Remo! *Por favor!* Help me!" It ended in a fleshy smack and a whimper.

There was no other way down, so Remo and Chiun simply waited, their eyes shifting between the looming entity on the summit and the approaching gunmen.

When they were within earshot, Remo called down.

"That's far enough. What do you want?"

Guadalupe started to speak. Her eyes focused upon the statue of Coatlicue. "What is that doing here?" she demanded fearfully.

"I think she means you," Remo told Mr. Gordons.

"I am here to negotiate for my survival," Gordons rumbled.

And Guadalupe Mazatl, hearing the stone voice of the Mother of the Sun, screamed.

She was flung aside. A corpulent man in a silk shirt and rings on his fingers shouted up.

"I have come to bargain for the life of the U.S. *presidente!*"

"Too late," Remo called back. "He's coming with us."

"I will double their offer," Jorge Chingar said. "I am El Padrino. I am very wealthy. I can make your every desire come to pass."

"Stuff it," Remo said. "We already have a deal. Right?"

Mr. Gordons spoke up. The snake heads peered down. *"I am promised the office of the Vice-President. What can you offer me?"*

El Padrino laughed. "They are lying to you, *amigo*. It is all a trick. They know you are Señor Gordon."

At that, the stones monster stepped off the summit, its clawed feet cracking the steps.

"Damn!" Remo said. He threw up his hands. "Okay, you got us. We know you're Gordons. But the deal's still on. We have authorization."

The idol lurched down, its ungainly arms flung out

for balance. The *pistoleros* of El Padrino clustered
about him protectively, their Uzis and Mac 10's trained
upward at the advancing colossus.

"It is too late to bargain," Chiun intoned. "We will
have to fight."

"No!" Remo said anxiously. "We waste Gordons, and
we've lost the President."

"Smith said that the President is better off dead
than in the hands of evil ones," Chiun said. "We first
of all must ensure our own survival."

Remo hesitated. "I'd love to debate this, but there's
no time," he said. "I'm with you."

Together they raced up to meet the lumbering
monster that was Mr. Gordons.

"Okay, Gordons," Remo challenged. "We tried to
do this your way. Now the gloves are off. We do this
our way or it's rock-garden time."

"You attempted treachery," Gordons said, the dismembered hands on his chest grasping like dying
spiders.

A blunt arm lashed out. Remo ducked. Not fast
enough. His reflexes were sluggish. One stone limb
connected with a glancing blow. Remo was sent stum-
bling backward.

But the blow left Mr. Gordons exposed on that side.

The Master of Sinanju angled in, one fist out. His
blow was solid. It chipped stone. The creature, off-
balance, rocked back from the impact.

It turned, a grinding stone automaton. Both arms
raised like pile drivers.

Landing on the terrace below, Remo recovered
quickly. His head hurt. He clambered to his feet,
the sight of the upraised arms descending on his
teacher galvanizing him to action.

Then the shooting started.

Bullets spanked off the pyramid side and steps. Remo whirled away from a stinging bullet track.

El Padrino's voice lifted.

"Cease fire," he called. "We are here to negotiate, not battle."

The upraised stone arms froze. The Master of Sinanju faded back from their menace.

Mr. Gordons turned his blocky body clumsily. The serpent heads looked down.

"I will listen to any reasonable offer as long as my survival is not threatened," he said.

"Señor Gordon, I can assure this," said El Padrino. "I am a very rich man. I own a fine hacienda that is like a fortress. I will see that no one injures you ever. I ask only that the President be handed over to me."

"Over my dead body," Remo growled.

A battery of Uzis suddenly pointed in Remo's direction.

"This can be arranged," El Padrino said simply.

"I do not want any deaths until the negotiations are finished," Mr. Gordons growled abrasively.

Remo turned to face him. "The vice-presidency still goes, Gordons. I can deliver."

"Do not be a fool, Gordon," El Padrino said. "Even if they agree to this preposterous thing, the Vice-President will be out of office in four years, perhaps eight. What guarantees do you have after this?"

"Is this true?" Gordons asked Remo.

"Hey, you could become President after that," Remo countered. "A lot of Vice-Presidents become President."

"This is true?"

"Sure," Remo said. "It's the American way. Anyone can become President. Right, Chiun?"

"I know this to be true, insane as it sounds," the Master of Sinanju intoned.

"You cannot possibly believe this, Señor Gordon," El Padrino cried. "With me, you have a lifetime yob. I have many uses for a yuggernaut such as yourself."

"I wouldn't take the word of a drug dealer," Remo pointed out. "Especially one with a speech inpediment."

"Is this true? Are you a criminal?"

"I am a businessman," El Padrino said smoothly. "In my country, I am more famous than the Vice-President. See my fine *pistoleros?* They would lay down their very lives for El Padrino. And for you, Señor Gordon, if I say this."

"Prove this. Have one lay down his life for you."

"Of course," El Padrino said. He nodded to Co-mandante Embutes, who yanked Guadalupe Mazatl to her feet. He put a gun muzzle to her temple.

"We will kill this one, hokay?"

Guadalupe looked up through the disarrayed hair over her face. Her brown eyes leaked tears.

"Oh, Coatlicue," she pleaded. "Do not let them kill your daughter. I implore you."

"Do it!" El Padrino ordered.

"No," said the Master of Sinanju. "There is a better way."

"What way is that?" asked Mr. Gordons.

"Ask the woman," Chiun said. "She is about to die. She knows us all. Ask her whom you may trust."

The serpent heads swept away from the Master of Sinanju to the woman, Guadalupe Mazatl.

"Tell me," Gordons rumbled.

"There is only one way you can know the truth," Guadalupe Mazatl said. "And that is by telling them all where the *presidente* is. Among my people, we have a saying. *Caras vemos, corazones no sabemos.* It means 'Faces we see, hearts we don't know.' "

"*Should I tear out their hearts?*" Mr. Gordons asked.

"No. It means that only by their actions can you judge them."

"The woman speaks wisdom," Chiun told Gordons.

The statue was silent. Its unwinking serpent eyes shifted from face to face. Then the heads rejoined with a clicking kiss so that the flat eyes looked out.

"The President is safe within the hollow ape atop the building called Banana," he said at last.

"Banana?" Remo said. Chiun shrugged.

"Banana?" El Padrino asked. Comandante Embutes snapped his fingers. "The monkey atop the Banana boutique. In the Zona Rosa. He is there!"

"*Gracias,*" El Padrino said, signaling to Comandante Embutes, who still had Guadalupe by the hair. He shot her through the temples once. Once was enough.

She slumped over, tumbling back down the steep steps like a broken doll.

"No!" Remo cried. He reached the steps in a single leap. One hand lashed out, ruining the *comandante*'s face. He kicked backward, taking out another *pistolero* with a toe to the throat.

El Padrino retreated as his men closed on Remo. Their pistols came up, fixing Remo in a crossfire. Remo ducked under a snapping bullet. He felt it go through his hair. He had been too slow, and the other muzzles were tracking for him.

Above, the Master of Sinanju turned to Mr. Gordons.

"You see your answer," he said. "Are we on the same side?"

"*Yes.*"

"Then prove your loyalty by helping my son."

Mr. Gordons serpent head snapped apart. He crushed down the stairs—heavy, ponderous, unstoppable.

As his golem shadow fell over the combatants, El Padrino turned. His face registered horror. He lifted his Uzi. Streams of bullets rattled out, pocking the stone hearts of Coatlicue's broad chest.

Still the monster came on.

Square pile-driver arms swept down, bursting human heads like melons.

Seeing *pistoleros* falling all around him, Remo Williams slid out of the melee. He took the opportunity to trip one *pistolero,* sending him over the side of the terrace. The gunman landed on the one below, every bone shattered.

El Padrino ran out of bullets. He made the sign of the cross and stumbled back for the steps. Remo plunged after him.

Mr. Gordons trampled one last *pistolero* who had stayed to fight, and began lumbering down the stairs.

El Padrino got as far as the next terrace. Looking over his shoulder, he saw Remo and, more frighteningly, Coatlicue descending, and ran for the stairs.

He made a mistake many tourists make. He ran for the stone markers he thought headed the next flight of steps.

El Padrino assumed his feet would hit the stairs running. It was a wrong assumption. There were no stairs. He ran off the side of the pyramid, falling fifty feet. He didn't scream until he hit the terrace. Then he bleated like a lamb tangled in barbed wire.

Remo skidded to a stop. He saw El Padrino lying there, his legs twisted at impossible angles. The drug king coughed blood, proving that he was still alive.

The Master of Sinanju floated to Remo's side, ahead of the descending Coatlicue.

"Now what?" Remo asked, watching Gordons clumsily negotiate the steps.

"See to Guadalupe," Chiun said. "Now!"

"What about Gordons?"

"Leave him to me," the Master of Sinanju said, turning to face Mr. Gordons.

Remo went, quickly disappearing from sight.

Mr. Gordons strode to the lip of the terrace. He looked over the edge to El Padrino's struggling body. He was atttempting to crawl to the steps. He left a trail of blood like a snail track.

"Well done, man-machine," said the Master of Sinanju, bowing.

"I am ready to return to America," said Mr. Gordons, clicking his serpent heads together. His walleyed gaze turned to regard the Master of Sinanju.

"You trust me, then?"

"Yes. Because of your actions. They tell me what your face and heart do not. At last I understand meat-machine behavior."

"Very wise. And I trust you too—unless of course you were lying."

"I was not lying. The President is hidden inside the ape."

"Excellent," Chiun said, pleased. His hands withdrew into his kimono sleeves. "Then we shall go to him as allies. After you have answered a question."

"What question?"

"When we last encountered one another," Chiun said, "my son Remo fought the thing he thought was you. And I attacked the globe which I believed contained your brain. Both died at the same instant. Which truly contained your brain?"

"It was in the satellite," replied Mr. Gordons.

"That was very clever. And creative."

Mr. Gordons inclined his broad head. *"Thank you. I pride myself on my creativity."*

"No doubt your brain is an equally creative place this time," said Chiun slyly.

"It is."

"My son, who guessed wrong once before, is convinced it is in your right serpent's head."

"He is wrong," said Mr. Gordons.

"But I am cleverer than he," Chiun went on, lifting a long-nailed finger. "I know that it is in your left head."

"Why do you think that?" asked Mr. Gordons.

"Because you are clever, and that is not only the most creative place for your precious brain but also the safest."

"It is?" asked Mr. Gordons.

"Yes," said the Master of Sinanju. "For most humans are what is called right-brained. Or logical. By making yourself left-brained, you are automatically more creative."

"One moment." Mr. Gordons stepped around in place. His thick legs required him to take small side steps to turn his ponderous stone body.

"Why do you turn your back on me?" Chiun asked politely.

"There is something I must do," Gordons said, bending at the waist. One hand lifted to his left hemisphere.

"I am glad you trust me enough to do this," Chiun said.

"I trust you because of your actions. They tell me you have negotiated in good faith."

"And your words tell me that you are a blockhead,"

said the Master of Sinanju as he set one sandaled foot to the serpent-twisted backside of the living statue of Coatlicue and exerted sudden force.

Mr. Gordons, in the act of transferring his brain from his left arm to his left hemisphere, toppled over the pyramid's side without a sound.

Landing, he broke into eight irregular pieces, pulverizing the still-squirming body of Jorge Chingar, a.k.a. El Padrino.

Remo came up the stairs like a rocket. He reached the shattered hulk that was Gordons. He looked up. "He's not moving."

"His left serpent's head is cracked in two," Chiun said as he floated down to join Remo.

"Yeah?" Remo said blankly.

"That's where his brain is," Chiun said smugly.

Remo looked at Coatlicue's fractured face. "How do you know that?" he wondered.

Chiun beamed like a wrinkled yellow angel. "The same way I know that it was I who killed Gordons last time, not you."

"How's that?" Remo said suspiciously.

"Because Gordon's told me so." And Chiun's angelic smile broadened.

"I don't believe it," Remo said as he knelt to examine the inert shattered hulk. Chiun kicked at it as if testing the tires on a used station wagon. Nothing happened. They separated the pieces, expecting a reaction. The statue of Coatlicue still didn't stir.

"See?" Chiun said happily. "Dong ding, the witch is dead."

"It's ding dong, and there's no sense in taking chances," Remo muttered, lifting one knifelike hand over Coatlicue's broken left facial hemisphere. "Let's pulverize it into rock dust." He brought the edge of his hand down hard.

To Remo's surprise, his hand bounced off, making a hairline crack.

"Damn!" Remo said. "You try it."

The Master of Sinanju kicked at the stone, knocking a tiny chip loose.

"It's that bad Mexican air!" Remo growled. "We're not up to speed."

Chiun frowned. "We cannot dawdle here, Remo. There is still the President to consider."

Remo hesitated, his eyes on the broken hulk.

"Okay," he said, getting to his feet. "The President first. But we're coming back to finish the job."

They pelted down the pyramid's side, stopping at the base, where Guadalupe Mazatl's dead body lay sprawled.

Remo knelt to close her brown eyes.

They ran to their car without a backward glance.

When the stifling gorilla head came off, the President of the United States was practically in tears. He blinked in the bright sun.

"Who's there?" he moaned. "I don't have my glasses. I can't see."

"Never mind," Remo assured him. "You're safe."

On the Banana boutique roof, they pulled the plaster-and-fur King Kong apart, extracting the President. Carefully they lowered him to the artificial jungle floor.

"Where am I?" the President asked in concern.

"Just close your eyes," Remo added. "We're taking you to the U.S. embassy."

"Thank God you came back," the President moaned.

Then he passed out. His last breathy exhalation sounded like "Dan."

Remo looked to Chiun. "He thinks we're—"

"Hush," said the Master of Sinanju as he folded the President's arms over his chest in preparation to move him. "It may be better this way."

The Vice-President of the United States didn't understand.

One moment, he was getting ready to read his speech, when the envelope containing it was wrenched from his hands.

"Never mind that," his chief of staff said quickly. "*Air Force Two* is waiting. The President wants you by his side. Now."

They bundled him into a waiting limo and to the airport.

Before he knew it, he was set down in Mexico City, where the President was ushered aboard by tense Secret Service agents.

The President looked ragged, but he smiled wanly.

"Dan," he said effusively. "Great to see you again— really wonderful." The Vice-President endured the firm two-handed handshake that seemed unending.

"Thank you, Mr. President," he said, wincing. His hand hadn't recovered from the morning's "grips-and-grins" marathon.

"Call me George," said the President. He turned to a steward. "Okay, on to Bogotá."

The Vice-President blinked blankly. " Bogotá?"

"We're going together, my boy." The President grinned. "From now on, we're a team. Where I go, you go."

"That's great," said the Vice-President, grinning weakly under his dazed blue eyes. He wondered what the hell had gotten into the President. He decided not to press his luck. Sheer dumb luck had catapulted him to the vice-presidency. No point in rocking the boat now. And maybe he'd get a little respect at last.

Although right now he would trade the vice-presidency for a bowl of hot Epsom salts for his aching hand. Why hadn't anyone warned him the job would be so demanding?

27

Remo and Chiun were relaxing in their air-conditioned room at the Hotel Krystal when the phone rang. Remo was on the bed. Chiun sat on the floor, poring over a book. Outside, it was raining again. Lightning lashed the skyline.

Remo picked up the phone. "Smitty?"

"It's all settled, Remo," Dr. Harold W. Smith said without preamble. "The President and Vice-President have arrived in Bogotá aboard *Air Force Two*."

"What about *Air Force One*?" Remo asked.

"That story is about to break. The White House is playing it as an air accident caused by pilot failure. The official NTSB report will attribute it to 'circadian desynchronosis.'"

"What the hell is that?"

"Jet lag."

"But Mexico City is only an hour behind Washington time," Remo pointed out.

"Nevertheless, that is the official story. We have to account for the dead."

Remo shrugged. "How's the President doing?"

Smith cleared his throat uncomfortably. "He believes the Vice-President is a latter-day Conan the

Barbarian. He will be allowed to go on thinking that. The Vice-President has been told by his handlers that the President is not quite himself as a result of surviving the crash landing, and to nod and smile at everything he says, no matter how puzzling."

"He's good at that, at least," Remo said dryly. "I suppose it's on to Colombia and killing a few loose ends for us?"

"No," said Smith. "One of the bodies discovered on the Pyramid of the Sun was Jorge Chingar, El Padrino—the man who had the contract on the President's life."

"No kidding," Remo said with pleasure. "I didn't want to go to Colombia anyway. All that's left is finishing with Gordons, which we'll do when we get back up to speed."

"Too late."

Remo's hand tightened on the receiver. "What do you mean?"

"The Mexican authorities have discovered the shattered Coatlicue statue. It's even now being crated for return to the Museum of Anthropology."

"No sweat," Remo said casually. "We'll hit it there."

"No, Remo. Better to let sleeping dogs lie."

"What do you mean?"

"It's an expression. It means—"

"I know that!" Remo snapped. "But what does that have to do with Gordons?"

"That idol, Remo, is a very important national Mexican symbol," Smith said levelly. "It was found on the site of Tenochtitlán, the ruined Aztec capital on which modern-day Mexico City has been built. Let the Mexicans put it together if they can, and restore it to its proper place in the museum."

"What if Gordons isn't dead?" Remo wanted to know.

"I think he is this time," Smith replied. "And if not, he will be well taken care of by the museum staff. Perhaps Gordons might grow to enjoy being a museum piece. No one will threaten his survival ever again."

"We're taking an awful chance," Remo warned.

"Our job is done. Return on the next flight."

"How about a 'Well done'?" Remo suggested.

The line went dead.

Remo stared at the receiver in his hand.

"How do you like that Smith?" he complained to the Master of Sinanju. "Not even a thank-you."

"Assassins are never appreciated in any age," Chiun said absently. He was paging through an oversize book entitled *The Aztecs*.

Remo put down the phone, smiling.

"Yearning for the glory days, Little Father?" he asked.

"It is a shame," said the Master of Sinanju. "These Aztecs were the Egyptians of their time. They had worthy kings, princes, and even slaves. Perhaps they may rise again."

"Count me out if they do," Remo said.

"We would have served true emperors, not temporary presidents and disposable presidents of vice," Chiun lamented. "We would have fitted in perfectly."

"Only if we wore oxygen masks," said Remo. And when he laughed, his lungs hurt.

28

Standing before the expectant crowd, which included the President of Mexico and other dignitaries, Mexican Museum of Anthropology curator Rodrigo Luján waited nervously as the last guest speaker finished introducing him. Behind him, perched on her basalt dais and bathed in multicolored spotlights, towered the massive tarpaulin-draped figure of Coatlicue.

It had taken a week of hard work by museum specialists to put the sundered pieces of Coatlicue together. They fitted remarkably well. The museum specialists had carefully restored her, using a special concrete paste to repair the bullet holes and knit the sections together. Steel bolts had been necessary to hold the bicephalic head together, but when Coatlicue was carefully raised to her clawed feet, she was whole.

A creditable job of restoration, but the hairline cracks were as if Coatlicue had been scored by stone-cutting machetes. It was sad. She would never again be the same.

The speaker finished. Rodrigo bowed at the mention of his name. With a sad heart, he pulled the tarpaulin free of the idol, revealing the brutal elemental beauty of the restored Coatlicue. A gasp of astonishment came from the assembled audience. Cries of "Bravo!" resounded. Rodrigo looked behind him. He gasped too.

For not a crack was visible on Coatlicue's ornate skin. Even the filled-in bullet holes were invisible. It was miraculous, as if the spirit of Coatlicue herself had taken hold of the stone, healing it until the idol was once again whole.

Rodrigo Luján bowed in acknowledgment of the applause that washed over him like thunder. But in his heart he gave silent thanks to Mother Coatlicue, whose ophidian eyes he felt on him.

For he was, above all things, Zapotec.